NINA BAWDEN

was born in London in 1925 and evacuated to South Wales during the war. She was educated at Ilford County High School for Girls and at Somerville College, Oxford.

Her first novel, *Who Calls the Tune*, appeared in 1953. Since then she has published nineteen other adult novels including: *Tortoise by Candlelight* (1963); *A Little Love, A Little Learning* (1965); *A Woman of My Age* (1967); *The Grain of Truth* (1968); *The Birds on the Trees* (1970); *Afternoon of a Good Woman*, winner of the Yorkshire Post Novel of the Year Award for 1976; *Familiar Passions* (1979); *Walking Naked* (1981); *The Ice House* (1983) and *Circles of Deceit*, which was shortlisted for the Booker Prize in 1988 and filmed by the BBC. Her most recent novel is *Family Money* (1991).

Nina Bawden is also an acclaimed author of sixteen children's books. Many of these have been televised or filmed; all have been widely translated. Amongst them are: *Carrie's War* (1973); *The Peppermint Pig*, the recipient of the 1975 Guardian Award for Children's Fiction; *The Finding* (1985), *Keeping Henry* (1988), *The Outside Child* (1989) and *Humbug* (1992).

For ten years Nina Bawden served as a magistrate, both in her local court and in the Crown Court. She also sat on the councils of various literary bodies, including the Royal Society of Literature – of which she is a Fellow – PEN, and the Society of Authors, and is the President of the Society of Women Writers and Journalists. In addition she has lectured at conferences and universities, on Arts Council tours and in schools.

Nina Bawden has been married twice and has one son, one daughter and two stepdaughters. She lives in London and in Greece.

Virago publish nine of Nina Bawden's works of fiction. *George Beneath a Paper Moon* is forthcoming.

VIRAGO
MODERN
CLASSIC
NUMBER
393

Nina Bawden

FAMILIAR PASSIONS

To Austen

Published by VIRAGO PRESS Limited February 1994
42–43 Gloucester Crescent, London NW1 7PD

First published in Great Britain by Macmillan London Ltd. 1979
Copyright © Nina Bawden 1979

A CIP catalogue record for this book is available from the British Library

Printed and bound in Great Britain by
Cox & Wyman Ltd., Reading, Berkshire.

Chapter One

Before James told his wife that he was leaving her, he took her out to dinner. It was their thirteenth wedding anniversary and he always took her out to dinner on their wedding anniversary. He had chosen this restaurant, he told Bridie, because it had been awarded a pestle and mortar symbol in the latest Good Food Guide. In fact his secretary had recommended it and made the reservation, as she always did. She had also bought the bottle of *Femme* that James always gave his wife on this occasion and put it, wrapped and ribboned, into his briefcase before he left the office.

Bridie Starr preferred *Ma Griffe* but she had never said so. James's first wife who had died, tragically young, in a car crash, had been fond of *Femme*. When James had married Bridie and brought her to his house, a matron at nineteen, a mother for his children, her predecessor's clothes had still been in the closet, her jewellery and toilet things still in the dressing-table drawer. Bridie understood, humbly, that James had been too upset to touch them. She gave the clothes away, but wore the jewellery and used the scent as James suggested that she should, insisting she loved *Femme*, to please him. To say that she preferred another perfume might seem not only hurtful but perverse, a childish desire to be 'different', and she wanted to appear grown up in James's eyes. By the time she realised that he had not been sensitive about poor Angel's sad belongings, merely lazy – tidying up, like booking tables and buying presents was not a man's job to his mind – it had been too late to retract her tenderly intentioned lie. He would have thought her foolish to have pretended in the first place. Devious, too – and James admired directness. Or said he did, and she believed him.

Happy marriages are full of small deceits, she thought, smiling at him across the table in this excellent, expensive restaurant. She hoped it wasn't *too* expensive. James wasn't stingy, but he hated to be rooked. She watched him anxiously as, monocle in eye, he scrutinised the bill. She saw him frown. 'It was a good meal,' she reminded him, adding, cunningly, 'And a double celebration after all! Two, for the price of one!' James liked a bargain. (His likes and dislikes were unremarkable and need not be remarked on here, except to say that to Bridie they were natural obstacles, like mountains in a landscape, and she constructed her life about them, living in the foothills, secretly, as a slave or child might do.)

'What? Oh, yes.' James took out his wallet and removed a credit card. He was still frowning as he made out the bill but in a vague, abstracted way – not so much at the bill, Bridie decided now, as at some inner thought, some doubt . . .

The British plastics firm of which James was commercial manager was merging with a Franco-German company and James had been invited to join the board of the new international company as marketing director. He had told Bridie over dinner and she was uncertain how he really felt about it. He had *seemed* delighted but she guessed he must be nervous, too; worrying about this new responsibility. She hadn't liked to ask him. He might have thought *she* thought he was getting old and past it. It occurred to her that even the tentative question she had put could be misinterpreted. He must have known about the merger for some time. To ask if he were 'pleased' about his appointment might suggest to him that she thought he may have feared he would not get it. (These tortuous considerations were as natural to Bridie as breathing. She did not know she was afraid of James. If she had been told she would have laughed.)

He said, 'Of course I'm pleased, you silly goose. Though there are some things we have to talk about. Not now. Later on, when we get home.'

He rose from the table and put her silk shawl round her shoulders. A tinted wall mirror reflected this courteous gesture. Looking into it, Bridie saw a handsome, prosperous couple: a tall man with sharp, distinguished features, a fresh-faced woman with wide, grave, brown eyes. James looked young for fifty and she looked old for thirty-two, she thought, not minding this, only pleased because she hoped he felt it flattered him. Their eyes met in the candle flicker of the glass. She said, 'That was a lovely meal. *Dear* James. Would you like me to drive home?' He looked at her long enough for her to wonder if he suspected there was some hidden condescension in her offer, some suggestion that he was too old, or too tired, or too drunk to take the wheel, before rewarding her with an open, generous smile and saying, 'Thank you, goose. I'm glad you've had a happy evening.'

He didn't speak throughout the hour's drive home. She thought he was asleep but when they crossed the river into the lit, empty streets of Westbridge, their Thames valley town, she glanced sideways and saw his eyes were open, gazing at her with a strangely mournful, fixed expression that didn't alter, even when she smiled at him.

She said, 'Had a good nap?' and, when he didn't answer, an uneasy feeling gripped her. How long had he been awake, without her knowing it, watching her with that clear, sad, and steady gaze? Why *sad*?

She felt a familiar anxiety; a pain in her heart, a heavy stone. Driving through the main street of the sleeping town, across the railway line and up onto Westbridge Hill, she sought a subject to divert and cheer him. She crossed the south side of the golf course and took a dark, winding, sylvan road, climbing past the Victorian water tower (subject of a preservation order), the famous pop star's house, the tennis club. She said, 'You know that foreign banker, what's his name, I never can remember? Van-Something. The one who has the private zoo. Apparently a stream runs through it into the lake at the back of the tennis club. The lake where the children used to swim. That's been stopped now. There's a notice saying that the lake's polluted. Do you know what with? With *tiger's pee*! Only the notice says *urine*, of course! But isn't it bizarre? In Surrey!'

She was glad to hear him laugh. More than glad, enormously relieved: the great, dull, aching weight had lifted from her chest. Absurd, she thought. *She* was absurd to feel this crippling anxiety for a grown man's happiness. Now, certainly. It was just a habit she had fallen into, early on. She had been anxious in those early days, with reason. He had been so unhappy when she met him, so lost and despairing. His first marriage had ended in a nightmare. Poor Angel, dragged unconscious from the wreckage of her car, rigged up to terrible machines for months, a breathing vegetable, a living death. Poor James, visiting her daily, had almost lost his reason. He had come to hate her, lying there so changed, and loathed himself for hating her. When Angel died, he had wanted to die too, to make amends. He had had frightening fantasies; dreamed, day and night, of throwing himself in front of trains, off cliffs. That was why he had gone to see Bridie's father, for professional advice, and it was in her father's consulting rooms that Bridie met him. She had been to the dentist to have a wisdom tooth extracted and Dadda had said that he would drive her home. He was busy with a patient when she got to Harley Street and James, just leaving, briefly introduced, had taken her round the corner to a pub and fed her aspirin and whisky. He had been concerned and kind but he had looked so sad, it wrung her heart. Forgetting her sore mouth and swollen cheek, she had coaxed him to talk about himself; tried, innocently, to cheer him up, and been so wonderfully relieved when he had smiled at last. That she, a girl in her last term at school, could ease this sad man's suffering amazed and awed her. He had said, 'You've done me more good than all your father's pills,' and she had felt so proud and happy. The habit of jollying him along had been formed then, she supposed, and become, like all habits, hard to break. She ought to try, she thought. If James was aware of it, he must find it burdensome . . .

She giggled almost silently, too low for James to hear, and turned into their driveway. Lights showed in several windows of the house and there was the sound of music playing.

The house was empty. An electrical device turned on lights and radio at irregular intervals. This wealthy, residential estate was good burglar country: badly lit, private roads, large houses in secluded, leafy gardens. Bridie said, as she got out of the car, 'I wonder if those tigers keep the villains off the banker's house. More effective, I should think, than our contraption.'

'That's only to keep the insurance people quiet,' James said. 'If you're nervous, you could get a dog.'

'I thought you didn't like dogs,' she said, surprised.

'Well . . .' He opened the front door and stood aside, punctiliously, to let her enter first. 'It was just a thought. Thank you for driving. I hope you're not too tired. Go on upstairs. I'll bring a drink.' He smiled at her. 'Champagne.'

She shook her head. Now he had mentioned it, she did feel tired. A lovely lassitude invaded her; she thought, luxuriously, of bed. 'Oh,' she said, 'I only really want to sleep.'

She guessed, seeing his knowing grin, that he assumed this was a sexual defence, He said, 'A shower will wake you up. And you can sleep late in the morning. I want to talk tonight.'

His smile had vanished now; his last sentence held a sudden, strained solemnity that made her mind leap to disasters. Her step-daughter, Aimee, eight months pregnant, had just lost her baby? Adrian, her step-son, had fallen off his motor bike; been picked up by the police for peddling drugs? Her daughter! Alarmed, she searched his face. That odd, sad look was in his eyes again. 'Not Pansy?' she cried. 'There's nothing wrong with Pansy?'

'No. What a goosey-girl you are! It's nothing like that. No

one is dead, or dying. Go on up and have your shower.'

He went down the passage to the kitchen. Obediently, she trailed upstairs, opened the window in their bedroom, peeled off her clothes and dropped them on the floor. Naked, she walked to the bathroom. Too lazy to shower, she washed her face and cleaned her teeth and dabbed *Femme* – from last year's anniversary bottle – on her breasts and wrists and throat. She put her nightdress on and brushed her short, coarse, curly hair, regarding her flushed, high cheek-boned face with a certain puzzled interest. She wasn't vain; she looked into the glass as young girls sometimes do, pondering and wondering. Is this really *me*, this arrangement of bone and eyes and skin and hair? There should be more *in* her face at thirty-two, she thought. Not sure what she meant by this, she looked, and sighed. At least her clear, dark brown eyes were beautiful. She wrinkled her nose at her reflection and said, aloud, 'You silly ass.'

James was waiting in the bedroom with the champagne and the glasses. He had already changed, in his own bathroom, into pyjamas and the quilted Chinese jacket she had bought at Liberty's and given him this morning. Above the mandarin collar, his narrow face was prim and dry. He said, 'You look very appetising like that, but won't you be cold, without a gown?'

Immediately, she wished that she had put one on. She felt her limbs exposed, like meat. A meal to tempt a husband's appetite; a well-hung pheasant, a ripe peach. She disguised her foolish irritation with a smile and joined him on the sofa beneath the open window. Half a mile away, one of the banker's tigers gave a lonely, coughing roar.

James poured champagne. He lit a black, Russian cigarette – his fifth, and last, today. Five daily cigarettes was, he considered, a reasonably calculated risk. He said, 'This job now. It will mean living abroad. Either Paris or Frankfurt. It's not decided yet.'

'Oh. You mean, altogether? Permanently?' She thought he watched her anxiously. Poor James! was he afraid she might not want to leave their house? She said, 'Darling, how exciting! And how marvellous that it should have happened now. I mean, last year, before Pansy went to boarding school, it would have been more difficult. But I can fly back for half term, that sort of thing, and she'll enjoy being abroad in the holidays. I must say, I rather hope it will be Paris, for her sake. Her French . . .'

He said, 'I don't want you to come.'

'What? Oh.' She laughed. 'I *see*. You mean, not now, at once. Of course there will be things to settle here. Do you want to sell the house or let it? When do we have to go?'

He said, loudly, 'I don't want you to come at all. I intend to live alone.'

She started. Then laughed again, so wildly that she spilled some of her champagne. Cold drops sprinkled on her naked thigh.

She said, in an absurdly bright, flirtatious tone, 'Do you mean you're leaving me?'

'I suppose you could put it like that.'

She blushed. Blushing, she held her cool glass to her burning cheek. She felt a terrible embarrassment. She said, 'Do you want a divorce?'

'No. No, I don't. I'll try to explain what I had in mind. But I imagine, really, that it will be up to you.'

He stopped and waited. She couldn't speak; her mouth had dried. Her tongue felt thick and rough. James said, with an air of mild reproach, 'This is very difficult for me. More difficult than I had anticipated.' He hesitated, then re-filled his glass. She held hers out. He filled it. He said, 'It would be insulting, I suppose, to say I'm sorry. And pointless, you may feel, to say I'm fond of you, although I am. We've had, I think, a happy and a useful life together. I hope you think so, too. The fact that I want to end it now doesn't take away from that. When couples separate, it's usual to assume that there must have been some fatal flaw in their relationship, that they are both to blame. In our case that isn't true, so I hope you won't look for something, to torment yourself. If it comforts you to blame *me*, I shall understand, although I hope, when you have heard me out, that you won't blame me too much. I know you have a generous heart. I think now – though in my defence I didn't think it *then* – that I took advantage of it when I married you. I blackmailed you with my sad widowhood, my children. Took advantage of your youth and generosity. The best years of your life, as your dear mother will doubtless comment when she hears.' His pale, tawny eyes – the colour of dry leaves – lit with sudden, sly amusement. 'I shall miss your mother and her original remarks.'

He paused – waiting for her to *smile*, she realised incredulously – then coughed.

She still said nothing: didn't dare to, now, in case she screamed aloud.

James looked at her ruefully. She saw he was disappointed that his little joke had fallen flat. After a brief interval he went on, speaking flatly, in a measured voice, like a chairman reading a company report. 'There are a couple of things I feel I ought to say. To sum things up. One is, that considered as a parental team, we haven't done too badly. Adrian's defection from the middle-class norm, though disappointing, is not unusual for the times we live in. Aimee is a flutter-brain but you were sensible enough to see that early on and discourage me from putting academic pressures on her that she couldn't handle. I know you don't like Dickie much, but marrying him was probably the best thing she could do and so far it seems to be working well. Pansy will be the most satisfactory of the three, I think. She has both intellect and character. I hope that pleases you, and it is certainly a great relief to me. After all, if I may say so, her birth was something of a gamble. Since you were an adopted child, I mean. I think it is fairly well established now that genetic factors are more important than environmental ones. I've never told you, but when you were pregnant I did have certain grave anxieties about how your offspring might turn out. I kept them from you, naturally.' He cocked his head on one side and raised one eyebrow playfully. 'That's *one* advantage of an elderly husband, that kind of emotional restraint! In fact, on the subject of my age, if I've taken the best years of your life there is a sense in which you've had the best of mine! I'm over the hill already. If we were to stay together, you might find yourself, ten years on or so, nursing a slipper'd pantaloon. Though that isn't why I want to go, of course.'

She said, attempting irony, 'I'm glad.'

He didn't seem to hear her. He was staring through the open window into the warm, scented, tiger-haunted night. When he spoke again, his voice had changed; become soft and reflective. 'There are so few real turning points. Times when you can change direction. If this chance hadn't come, I suppose I'd have gone on, trudging along the same old tram lines to the grave. But it has come, and I want to take it. This is the hardest part, explaining why. If a man jumps off a bridge, it's not because the bridge is there. He must have wanted to, beforehand. Perhaps that isn't a very good analogy. I want to live, not die. I believe my impulse to end our marriage is a healthy one, though I daresay your father would dispute that. Produce some bland, psychiatric term for my condition, prescribe some palliative pill. I can't tell you what I'm suffering from. All I can do is tell you what it feels like. I wake up in the mornings and feel that nothing lies ahead. Nothing but emptiness and death. Not intellectually – God knows, *I* know I have enough to do – but in my *guts*. I look at the sky and the grass and feel an unbearable sadness. As if the earth were weeping. I look at you, and you can't help me.' He turned from the window and regarded her with conscious, gallant brightness. She saw his eyes were full of tears. 'I know the cure. I have to get away. To be alone.'

She didn't believe a word of this. She said, 'You mean, with someone else?'

'Don't be so fucking vulgar!'

His sudden change from elegiac sentiment to anger shocked and frightened her. She shrank back as he shouted, slammed down his glass. His eyes – tearless now – glared like golden lamps. She thought – *a tiger's eyes*! 'You see?' he raged. 'You can't share this. You can't begin to understand or you would never have made that crude and cruel remark. You understand nothing. Nothing, *nothing*! All these months I've been in such despair. You've been kind to me, but I've come to loathe your kindness! Time and time again, I've seen you thinking, *poor old man*! Trying to keep me alive, that's what your kindness means. Watching me when I pour out a second glass of brandy after dinner, buying me margarine instead of butter. Treating me like a cracked old piece of china. Or like a useful machine you're keeping in repair. A good husband, a good provider, is that all I am?' He rocked backwards and forwards, moaning. 'I want to be something else before I die.'

She wondered if he were very drunk. All that wine at dinner, several brandies afterwards, and now, champagne. Or was he going mad? He had been working far too hard, coming home late at night, going to the office some weekends. She thought of one of her father's not-so-silly jokes. *Work is the ruin of the thinking classes*. She choked back a fearful laugh and said, 'I'm sorry.'

He controlled himself, making an obvious, physical effort; breathing in deep, painful gulps, clasping his hands together. He said, 'God. Oh God, I'm sorry. I didn't mean to lose my temper or reproach you. In the circumstances, I hardly have a right to!' Amazingly, he smiled at her, shyly and slyly; boyishly contrite. He unclasped his hands and stroked back his thinning hair. 'Dear Bridie, silly little goose, I've made such a mess of this. The main thing, what I wanted, was for us to part in friendship. In a civilised manner. The trouble is – or was – that I had no idea quite what my *tone* should be. Lugubrious, or business-like, or angry. How best to pitch it! If I've sounded like a lousy actor, it's because I've had no chance to play this role before. Perhaps I should just have written you a letter, setting out the terms I wanted us to part on, and given you a chance to think them over privately and quietly. As I've said, I don't want a divorce. What I would really like, would be for you to stay here, in this house, as my wife. If you agreed, there would be no tiresome bother over money. Apart from the fact that it seems I am to be paid, by British standards, a simply *huge* amount, I shall have to come back to London fairly regularly, for conferences, and as the firm would obviously pay all my expenses on those occasions, they might well pay something towards the upkeep of this house. Indeed, if you were prepared to put up the occasional foreign colleague I might bring with me, it's possible that I could wangle some sort of salary for you, as a kind of official housekeeper. I can't promise anything, but if you were agreeable, I could look into it. You need not be lonely here. I should never, of course, enquire into the life you led, the friends you made. And I thought I would perhaps buy you a dog. You've always wanted one.'

She picked up the champagne bottle and emptied it into her glass. Her head buzzed as she drank; her lips felt tingling numb, as if her mouth had been injected with cocaine.

He said, 'It wouldn't be too bad a life, would it? In fact, if you could make the adjustment, it could be pleasant for us both. For myself, selfishly, I'd like to feel I could come back sometimes. Come *home*! Not as a husband, unless you were willing, but as a loving friend. We could spend weekends together, part of Pansy's holidays! Celebrate family occasions as we have always done. You've always been so good at that. Birthdays, Easter, Christmas – you've always made them something special!' There was a damp shine in his golden eyes. 'I've always loved your Christmases,' he said.

The absurdity of this remark convinced her that he must be mad. Or she must be. She stood up and realised that she was, simply, very drunk. The room reeled round her. She said, politely – hearing her own small, polite voice from a long way off – 'I'm sorry, James, I can't go on. I'm sorry if it seems like an evasion, but I really must lie down.'

She staggered across the room and fell, prone, on the bed. Springs twanged as James sat down beside her. He said, 'Poor goose, I didn't realise. Do you feel very awful? Could you try and be sick, do you think? You'd feel better if you could be sick.

I'll help you to the bathroom.'

'No,' she groaned. 'No. Please. Just let me lie. I'll be all right if I can just lie still.'

She lay on her side, eyes closed. The bed was like a softly swelling sea, gently rocking her. Waves of sweat, and sleep, engulfed her. She felt James lifting her, lifting her legs, covering her with the cool sheet. She heard him say, 'I'll put a bowl beside you in case you feel sick in the night.'

It was the last thing she heard before she slept.

She woke to find him on top of her, between her legs, plunging into her. Not roughly, not hurting her – in her sleep she must have responded, opened to him, a co-operative, damp vessel. Awake, she stiffened angrily, twisted her head away. He said, into her ear, 'Relax, goose, and enjoy it.'

She lay inert, eyes closed. She felt a distant, tickling pleasure. She thought – What an extraordinary arrangement! She opened her eyes and saw, in the faint, morning light, his face above her, stripped of identity in this clumsy exercise. His mouth was slightly open, showing the gold fillings in his teeth. He grunted and collapsed between her breasts. He muttered, 'A pleasure for me, if not for you,' then laughed and rolled away. He gave an energetic, noisy yawn. 'Bridie, love,' he said. 'Bridie Starr. A pretty name. At least I gave you that, if nothing else. If it wasn't for me, you'd still be Mary Mudd.'

She stretched her legs; crept, shaking, to the extreme edge of the bed; lay still. After a little while she said something she had often longed to say. 'I wish you wouldn't make such stupid jokes.'

He didn't answer. She raised herself upon her elbow and saw he was asleep. The room was greyly lit; a grey and raining dawn. Rain tinkled in the gutters, whispered in the garden, splashed through the open window. She got up to close it and found the sill was wet. She went to the bathroom to fetch a towel to mop it up; stood, towel in hand, and said, aloud – though softly – 'What the hell!' She mopped herself, between her legs, threw the towel away, glanced up and saw her pale reflection grimacing in the mirror. A ghostly, white, and frightened face. Regarding it, she sighed, and shook. She whispered to it, 'You don't have to stay, you know,' as if consoling a scared child.

The words came unbidden, without conscious thought, but as soon as she had spoken them she understood why she had addressed herself like this, as if she were someone younger and weaker than she was. It was the only way she could force herself to act. The habit of protecting others was so strong in her. But there was no one else to be considered now, no child asleep in an adjoining room (as until these last few months there had always been), not even an animal to make arrangements for. She thought of James's offer to buy a dog for her and gritted her teeth and hissed with rage, watching her face miming resentment in the glass. She said, 'Get on with it, you fool,' and was, at once, spurred on, and terrified.

She tore her nightdress off, opened the airing cupboard (even though the door into the bedroom was closed, her heart pounded at the *click* of the magnetic catch) and pulled out jeans, underwear, a woollen shirt. Walking shoes and raincoat were in the downstairs cloakroom. She thought – *What else?* – and an absurd, irrelevant memory seized her suddenly. One year, when she had been a little girl, at school, she and a small group of friends had been obsessed by what they had called the Disaster Game. This game (played secretly, when no adults were near) had occupied long, argumentative, excited, fearful hours. What would they do if horror struck; a hurricane, an earthquake, a bomb, a burning house? How would they escape, where would they hide? What would they take with them? This practical problem had reduced their fears to comfortable proportions. They packed survival kits in satchels and discussed the contents at great length. Toothbrushes and money boxes and tins of Heinz Baked Beans had figured largely. They made a rule that each of them could take one book, one favourite toy, one piece of jewellery that could be used, they solemnly decided, for barter if times grew really hard. Bridie's choice had been a coral bracelet, a tenth birthday present (they had all been nine or ten, these little girls) and dressing now to leave her husband, clumsy-figured in her haste and fear, she remembered that she had it still. Where was it? This talisman, this token? Ridiculous to search for it, of course, but she was sure she'd seen it recently . . .

Since she had to pass through the bedroom, anyway, she would look in her jewel box. But as she opened the door, James muttered and rolled over. She held her breath and stood quite still until she heard his steady snore. It was too dangerous to look for her bracelet, she decided. Not that she was *afraid* of James! Not of his anger; not even of his mockery. How comic he would think this dawn departure; how irrational, how unnecessary, how *demeaning*! As if she were a servant girl who had been dismissed for pilfering the silver! Why he affected to despise servants she didn't know; she only knew this was the identification he would make. 'He always puts you in the wrong somehow.' In her mind she heard her step-son's young and sulky voice. Why had she thought of Adrian? *Of course* – the children's photographs! On her bedside table where they always stood, in a folding leather frame . . .

Adrian at twelve, the age she had first known him; his slyly secretive, sweet face. James had made him secretive with his sarcasm, his scorn. Aimee, younger, smiling with gap-toothed coquettishness had known better how to cope with James; she wasn't as stupid as he thought her. And Pansy, whose intellect and character he so admired, taken at eleven, before she went to boarding school. A handsome girl; bold, self-possessed, and strong. Bridie crossed the room; picked up the folder. The children's faces sustained and calmed her. It came to her with the force of something she had always known but only now acknowledged, that they were the only reason she had stayed so long; their pictures, the only thing she wanted to take with her.

She left the bedroom and her sleeping husband; left his house. The rain was easing; no more than a pleasant coolness on her cheeks. Wearing her old gardening raincoat, her old gardening shoes, she set off down the drive. Unlike most of the families on Westbridge Hill they only had one car (for environmental reasons, James maintained) and James would need it to get to the station. Usually Bridie drove him and picked up their daily cleaner afterwards but Mrs Tomkins was in hospital this week, having her womb dilated and curetted. A fortunate coincidence, this seemed to Bridie, suddenly. Except for James, no one's routine would be disturbed by her defection. She would send flowers to Mrs Tomkins and a note enclosing a month's wages. If James needed household help he would have to make his own arrangements . . .

No one was about, so early in the morning. Bridie walked, unobserved, beneath the dankly dripping laurels, avoiding, since she was on foot, the pop-star's hide out which was defended by roaming, savage dogs, and taking instead a slightly longer route that led past the banker's house. His tigers, unlike the pop-star's slavering Alsatians, were safely caged. She had seen them earlier this summer when, with a neighbouring American woman whose husband worked in the same merchant bank, she had used his swimming pool.

It had been a hot afternoon. They had swum and sun bathed by the pool which was in a carefully designed, exotic setting, adjacent to the zoo. The tigers had been sleeping in the summer heat until one was disturbed by a sparrow that had got into its cage somehow and fluttered to and fro, swooping above the tiger, almost touching it, then soaring to beat frantic wings against the bars. The tiger swished its tail and crouched as if springing to attack the bird, but it became obvious, as they watched, that the poor beast was terrified. It growled, weaving its heavy, handsome head; sank, trembling, to the ground. They laughed at first – its fear was so ridiculous – then grew concerned. The tiger's flanks were heaving in and out like bellows. Suppose it had a heart attack? There was no one to help; no keeper evident about the grounds. They searched the cage and saw, high up, a hole in the wire mesh of the roof through which a small bird might have entered. Hoping to drive it out again they banged the wire and shouted but the noise only made the bird fly wildly round the cage and alarm the tiger more. It rolled its eyes up and cowered in a corner, moaning, a low, pathetic, exhausted sound, deep in its throat. Above it, clinging to the wire, the bird looked down, head cocked enquiringly. They had gone guiltily away and left them; the trapped bird, the frightened tiger . . .

This incident seemed to Bridie now both comic and revealing. She and the American, both married to rich and comparatively elderly men, had both thought, at the same time, of heart attacks! Was that why they had both been so anxious for the tiger, not cared about the bird? Perhaps power brought low and caged was always pitiful. At least the bird, if it could find its hole again, was free to fly!

Bridie laughed into the rainy wind. She said, loud and clear, 'Don't be so bloody fanciful.' And laughed again at her stupid habit of talking to herself. A sign of madness, or of loneliness? 'Better run, you'll catch your death,' she said in an old woman's scolding voice. The cool rain felt chilly now; her shoulders and her feet were icy cold. She jog-trottted down the Hill, through white gates onto the London road and flagged down a passing van.

The van driver asked her where she wanted to be set down. Anywhere in London, she told him cheerfully and then remembered that she had no money. How stupid James would think her if he knew! 'Actually,' she said with an apologetic smile, 'I'm going to Belgravia.'

He looked at her curiously. Did he think her too bedraggled, in her old coat and muddy shoes, to be living in this expensive area? It seemed courteous to offer some kind of explanation even if, in the circumstances, she preferred to give a false one. Assuming a foreign accent – only a slight one, because she had not spoken this way until now – she told him she was an *au pair* girl from Sweden. She had spent the night with a friend, another Swedish girl, and had to get back to her employer's house in time to give the children breakfast.

The driver said, 'I thought all Swedish girls were blonde,' and laughed.

'Well,' Bridie said. 'Well. I'm not Swedish by birth, only by nationality. My parents are Polish in origin. They went to Sweden just before the war.' She was surprised how glibly this lie tripped off her tongue. Though it might not be a lie, she thought. After all, she didn't *know*, did she? All her parents had told her was that she had been an orphan, a war baby . . . 'Poles,' she added, for good measure, 'are often dark-skinned and dark-haired.'

The driver grunted. Like Bridie, he had only spoken from politeness. He had not wanted, nor expected, this fulsome explanation in return for a simple act of kindness on a wet and dreary morning. He said no more, asked no more questions, and when they got to London dropped her off at Hyde Park Corner. The rain was heavy when he left her, darkening the sky and swirling in the gutters. Passing cars and taxis splashed her. She had dried out in the van driver's heated cab, but by the time she had walked to Eaton Square she was, again, wet through. She arrived on the doorstep of the tall, imposing house in which her parents had a penthouse flat, weary, moneyless and sodden-footed, like a waif in a Victorian melodrama. Only the children's photographs, clutched against her chest beneath her ancient raincoat remained moderately dry. Her survival kit, she thought, as she pressed the bell and leaned, yawning, against the door post, waiting for the automatic buzzer; her testimonial for thirteen years hard labour.

Chapter Two

'Thirteen years,' Hilary Mudd said. 'Taking your young life and using it, making a convenience of you, a nanny and a housekeeper, then throwing you away like a sucked orange! A worn out glove!'

Standing at the foot of her parents' double bed, raincoat dripping on the fluffy carpet, Bridie smiled. How James would laugh if he could hear these tired old phrases – what he had called her mother's 'original remarks.' How *dare* he laugh, she thought, remembering with shame how she had once laughed with him. How sycophantic she had been, how treacherous, how *ignorant*! Her mother simply spoke as she thought and felt, innocently using, in pain or happiness, the words others had used before. And why not? The crucial human situations never changed . . .

Her mother said, 'And on your wedding anniversary, too. What a wicked time to choose. How cruel!'

'Oh, Muff. *That* doesn't matter. Truly! And for the rest – well, I really think he must be ill.'

'Rubbish. The man's a monster,' her psychiatrist father confidently said. He gave his short, loud laugh; his cheeks kindled with their ready flush. 'Always thought so, I can tell you now! Ever since he let his frightful mother call you *Bridie*! James's bride! Bloody condescending. Bloody awful cheek, I thought.'

'Oh, Dadda! It was only because her name was Mary, too. I didn't mind.' Bridie looked at her parents helplessly; at Muff, sitting pillow-propped in bed, at Dadda, erect and taut and angry in his old, grease-spotted dressing-gown. His face (the face of a small owl, or hawk) had shrunk and tightened with the years; her mother's had sagged and softened, skin hanging from her bones in soft and powdery pouches. Bridie, who loved them, was saddened every time she saw them by each new, small sign of age; longed to protect, to spare them. Instead, this morning, she had brought them pain. She said, to make amends, to make them smile, 'You know, James thinks he did me a tremendous favour, changing my name from Mary Mudd. It was the very last thing he said to me.'

Her father snorted. Her mother closed her eyes and sighed.

Bridie said, 'Darlings, it's not so terrible. Don't be hurt for me, because *I'm* not! Really, the odd thing is, I don't think I care so very much. Not at the moment, anyway. I just feel a fool, that's all. *Ashamed.* I can't explain it.'

'Ridiculous!' her father said.

'You've done nothing to be ashamed of,' her mother cried. 'Oh, that man! He should be horse-whipped!' She clenched her small and pretty hands. Beneath her chin, the soft flesh shook with passion.

Bridie laughed. 'At least I'm free of him. At least he made it easy! Even if I didn't know that's what I wanted, I think I *almost* know it now. As if some spell was lifting.' This was really how she felt, she thought. She had woken from some long, enchanted sleep and returned to life like Rip Van Winkle; finding her parents older, but otherwise unchanged. Still Muff and Dadda – how those silly, childish names had clung; how sweet they sounded to her! She said, 'Please, Muff, don't be too upset. It's bad for you, so early in the day. You haven't even had your breakfast yet.'

'I was just about to get it,' her father said. 'Take off those wet things and hop into bed with Muff. I'll bring a tray.'

'You'll find a robe behind the bathroom door,' her mother

said. 'A new pink one I bought the other day in Harrod's. Nice,
soft alpaca. There's nothing like wool, I always think. Have a
hot shower, my darling, and don't forget to dry your hair.'

Stripping in the bathroom, obediently towelling her wet hair,
breathing in her mother's scent as she slipped on her mother's
robe, Bridie felt returned to childhood. Breakfast in her
mother's bed had always been a special treat. Muff rarely got
up before eleven now (after a mild heart attack last year she
needed extra rest) but she had always breakfasted in bed because Dadda liked to make it for her, bringing to this morning
task an almost priestly sense of ritual. It was his working class
background coming out, he said; in the mining family he came
from the men always lit the range fire in the mornings and took
their wives a cup of tea in bed before leaving for the early shift.
Martin Mudd had never gone down a mine, never worked with
his hands, but it pleased him, preparing soft-boiled eggs, thin
toast and China tea, to feel he was acknowledging his social origins. He had told Bridie once, 'My father used to get me up
after he had lit the fire. He'd put up a sheet of tin to draw the
flame and when he took it away the heat was fit to roast an
ox. I used to sit by the fire to get my homework done before
the others woke. There was no peace in our house at any
other time. My father had a great respect for education,
worked himself to death to keep us all at school. Those
mornings, when I was studying for my scholarship and he
made the tea, were the only times we were alone together.
We never talked. Often now, I wish we had. He was a nice
man.'
  This was the only time Bridie had ever heard him admit to
tender sentiment about any member of his family which was
large, boisterous and belligerent, united only by what sometimes seemed a terrible anger against the world, expressed in
epic quarrels which would need a Homer, Martin said, to
chronicle effectively. Although time had reduced their numbers, there were five children, numerous cousins and two

ancient aunts still living. When they met (at weddings, fune-
rals) there was usually a bare half hour of smouldering civ-
ility before insults began to be exchanged, old injuries
remembered. 'Oil and water don't mix', Hilary Mudd said,
speaking of the conflict between Martin's father's family from
Norfolk, who were mild-mannered but secretive and stubborn,
and the witch's cauldron of Welsh blood that they had married
into. The Norfolk strain preferred to brood and keep their skeletons in cupboards; the Welsh dragged them out and bran-
dished them. When Bridie had been young it had alarmed and
fascinated her when aunts and uncles came and raged; astonished her to hear her father, so gentle always with his wife and
daughter, raise his voice and shout abuse. Considering how
much he affected to dislike his surviving brother and his sisters,
it was amazing how close he seemed to them on these occasions,
how passionately he recalled the memories they had in common. Affection did not come into it, perhaps, only a sense of
family, of physical likeness (all the Mudds had small heads,
luxuriant hair, bad teeth) – of blood being thicker than water,
as Hilary Mudd might say. Only she would never say it, Bridie
thought. Not to her adopted child . . .

Wrapped in her mother's new, pink, alpaca robe, thinking of
her mother, Bridie felt tears rising in her throat. Dear Muff, so
loving and so conscientious; so, simply, *good*. A form of goodness that might appear soft on the surface, a matter of manners,
of being kind, polite, not hurting others, but sprang, in fact,
from an inner, iron discipline. Muff was a Christian who saw
her faith not as a virtue but a gift, given her by God and nur-
tured by her father who had been a clergyman in the East End
of London and bore (so Martin said) a close resemblance to the
kindly deity she trusted in. She was also naturally generous and
sweet-natured. Although she led her own life according to strict
and simple rules, she rarely judged other people unless they
had offended someone that she cared for. She was not all milk
and water. When Martin met her, in the early nineteen-thirties,
she was working as a district nurse, in her father's parish. She

was visiting a pregnant woman whose husband was notorious for his temper. He had come home drunk and attacked his wife while Muff was there, punching her and cursing, and Hilary Mudd, seizing the nearest implement that lay to hand, had beaten him about the head, split his forehead open, and sent a neighbour running to the nearest hospital. Martin, on casualty duty, had come at once. 'An amazing sight,' he told Bridie, who loved to hear this story. 'That great, drunken lout, cowering and bleeding in a corner, and Hilary standing over him with a rolling pin! Just what she would choose, of course!'

Martin had been a junior houseman then, intending to specialise in psychiatry. They married as soon as he was registered, lived for some years in a house in the grounds of an old mental asylum, had a daughter, Grace, who had died in 1943, a year before Bridie had been born and her parents had adopted her. 'Not as a replacement, darling,' her mother told her when she was old enough to understand. 'We wanted you for *yourself*. I only wish you could have known your sister. I'm sure you would have loved her, she was so sweet, Grace by name and grace by nature. We were lucky to have had her with us, even for so short a time. I wish poor Dadda could see it that way, that she was only lent to us, not given. It would make him happier, I know. He was so bitter when she died. It hurts him so much, still, even to talk about her.'

Bridie had had a happy childhood and believed that it was largely her mother's doing. Martin Mudd was clever, wayward, tortured; it was his wife's simplicity and strength that had kept the marriage firm. While she was growing up Bridie had seen this; watched her mother contain and calm her father without quite seeing how she did it, or recognising her father's part: his instinctive, warm response. What had entered into Bridie in those growing years was an understanding that this was a woman's proper role, to comfort and sustain a man. Was this, she wondered now, why she had married James? To emulate her mother? If she couldn't look like Muff, as at one time she had longed to – dreaming, in her adolescence, that she would wake one morning and find her strong, dark, gipsy looks miraculously transformed into her mother's fragile fairness – she could be like her in other ways; do for James, for that cold, aggrieved, unhappy man, what Muff had done for Dadda?

What presumption, she thought forlornly, yawning at her tired reflection in the steamy mirror. And what waste! Trying for thirteen years to force herself into a pattern that wasn't hers by nature. She wasn't like her mother, never had been, never could be. Muff's goodness was a simple, joyful thing; a gift bestowed upon her in her cradle. Trying to act like her, Bridie had been copying the shadow, not the substance; a brave attempt, she told herself, quite honourable, but false . . .

Admitting this, she felt a surge of sturdy cheerfulness. Smiling, she saw her reflected face smile back and thought she looked much younger suddenly. Tired, but smoothed out and calm. The relief of leaving James, perhaps? Oh, that was such pure relief! A prisoner, set free! Was that really all she felt? She frowned, considering. Surely there should be some other emotions more suitable to this occasion? Some unhappiness, some guilt – after all, however badly James had behaved last night, she must have failed him in some vital way! *Poor James*, she thought remorsefully, calling upon the anxious tenderness she had always felt for him. It did not come. She thought – *What's wrong with me*? She called upon her love for Pansy, for Adrian and Aimee, and was reassured to find it welling up as warm and strong as ever. It was only her husband she felt nothing for. Not even anger or resentment. She tested this. She said, aloud, 'I've always loved your Christmases.'

And laughed.

The telephone rang while they were eating breakfast. Tucked up in her parents' bed, Bridie gasped, and spilled her tea. Her mother took her cup and set it on the tray. 'Dadda will answer it, don't worry, darling.'

Martin left the room. He closed the door but his wife and daughter could hear his voice, sharply raised and angry, barking from his study across the tiny hall. Hilary Mudd mopped at the tea stain on the sheet with a lacey handkerchief. Bridie said, 'If it's James, I ought to speak to him,' and was aware, at once, that the idea excited her. Straining to hear her father's voice, distinguish words, she felt a trembling, exalted energy. Oh, the things that she could say to James now that she was safely free of him; free from his stupid jokes, his bullying, his self-regarding arrogance. The insults she could fling! Not in anger, but for pleasure . . .

Muff put a small, warm hand on hers. 'Poor lamb, you're shaking. Don't be frightened, darling, of course you haven't got to speak to him. You've been hurt enough, sufficient unto the day, and it won't do James any harm to hear from Dadda what we think of him. You've had so much to bear! I hope it's some small comfort that Dadda and I are here to help you bear it. You mustn't try to spare us. A trouble shared is a trouble halved, I always think. And I do understand a little of what you're going through. Another woman always understands. Especially a mother. When you said you felt ashamed, *I* knew. It went straight to my heart like a dagger and for a minute I really believe I felt your pain! It was so like you to try and take the blame. My tender, generous girl.'

Bridie shook her head, protesting. Her mother pressed her hand. 'Don't be too brave, my darling. It only makes it harder. Let your grief come.'

'I'm not . . .' Bridie began, but was silenced by the anguish in her mother's eyes. Muff was suffering on her behalf but she would suffer more if she thought she had a heartless daughter. Bridie attempted a wavering, wan smile and bent her head to hide a guilty blush. Muff said, 'My lamb,' and put her arms around her, drawing her down to lie against her breast. Although her neck was twisted at an awkward angle, Bridie submitted to this fond embrace. She murmured, 'It may not be James, of course.'

'There's no one else Dadda is likely to speak to in that tone of voice,' her mother said. 'Only his family, and they seldom ring so early. It costs less later in the day and they prefer to quarrel at cheap rates.'

She gave a surprising, sudden giggle and relaxed her loving hold. Bridie sat up gratefully and rubbed her neck. Her mother said, 'Oh dear, I shouldn't laugh.'

Bridie smiled. 'Is there a row on at the moment?'

'Florence has something brewing, I believe. Dadda spoke to her last night. Hammer and tongs for nearly half an hour. I don't know how he keeps it up. You'd think he'd be worn out.'

Bridie said, 'It's like a good brisk walk to him. Gets his circulation going.'

It was the first time she had identified her father's need; the healthy vein of coarseness in him that must be exercised. When he came into the bedroom, ruddy-cheeked, bright-eyed, she felt her own pulse stir in sympathy and quicken. She said, 'Well, Dadda?'

Martin grinned and cracked his finger joints. 'That was his Lordship. I think I saw him off. Is my wife there? *My wife*, you see. His property! *My daughter* has arrived, I told him. Sorry, he said. Sorry you've been troubled. Like some bloody telephone operator. I didn't comment at that point. Give him rope to hang himself, I thought, let him have his say. All more in sorrow than in anger – that was the line he took. Deeply shocked, poor fellow, to wake up and find his wife had sneaked off like a guilty servant – what's he got against servants, by the way? He'd hoped she would have had more dignity! He'd tried to be civilised and intends to go on trying, you'll no doubt be glad to hear. Make what he calls a reasonably generous settlement. You note the cagey adjective! Of course the house is in his name but since *his wife* has made it clear by her abrupt departure that she doesn't wish to live in it, he'll put it on the market. A proportion of the price it fetches will be put into a trust. Capital tied up for Pansy. There will also be a fair division of what – I quote – *might be seen as joint possessions*! Certain items of furniture, bed linen, kitchen equipment, cutlery. Not his family silver,

naturally! And there are some pieces of jewellery that belonged
to his mother. He mentioned a diamond and ruby ring. Value
and sentiment pretty closely linked, I think you'll find. But he
might consider giving up the car . . .'

Bridie laughed. Her father looked at her, with sudden, startled recognition. He said, 'I cut him short then. I said, don't
worry, we'll take you to the cleaners.'

'Please, Martin,' Muff said, 'Dearest, don't go on. I know
how you must feel, so angry on our poor child's behalf. That
monstrous man! But he is her husband! This must break her
heart.'

'I hardly think so,' Martin said.

Still laughing, Bridie said, 'I'm sorry, Muff.' She thought –
why am I apologising? She tried to think of something, some
statement her mother would find acceptable. 'I did love him
once. At least, I think I did. But it really has quite gone.'

Muff searched her face. 'Oh my darling, he has hurt you so!
You must hate him for it. Don't take a penny from him! There's
no need. Blood money!'

Martin snorted. 'Call it redundancy pay. It makes the situation clearer.'

Bridie said gently, 'I don't hate him, Muff. I don't even dislike him. I feel *indifferent*. Really, that's the truth. And while he's
welcome to his silver, I don't see why he shouldn't support me
for a little while. I shall have to live. I'll get a job, of course, but it
may take time to find something suitable. Something where I
can be free for Pansy in the holidays. I'm not qualified for anything.'

'Whose fault is that?' Her father rounded on her suddenly.
Blood mounted in his cheeks. 'You could have gone to university. It wasn't altogether James's fault you didn't. You can't
blame him for everything. You didn't have to marry him
straight out of school. A man old enough to be your *father*, for
God's sake! I told you at the time. Get a degree first, I said.
Some kind of training, anyway. Give yourself a breathing
space. But oh no, you wouldn't listen!'

Muff said, 'She loved him, Martin dear. And it wasn't only James who needed her. There were the children.'

'Sentimental nonsense! They weren't her responsibility.'

Bridie was astonished by his tone. Her anger leapt to answer his. 'I don't see that it was sentimental to have *cared*! I wanted to do something worthwhile with my life.'

'Rubbish. You were determined to sacrifice yourself. Romantic notions of a masochistic girl!'

'Martin dear, don't rage at her like that,' Muff said. 'Dearest, this isn't like you!'

'Don't worry, darling,' Bridie said. 'It cheers him up to shout at me.'

It cheered her up to shout back, too, but before her mother's loving, puzzled gaze, this was harder to admit. She smiled and said, 'It's easier than crying over spilt milk, after all.'

She was amazed how calm she felt. It couldn't last, she thought. The numbness would wear off soon, like an anaesthetic, and the pain would start. She almost hoped it would. It was unnatural to feel so composed and happy in these circumstances. So free and clear of all responsibility. Unnatural, certainly, for the sort of person she had always believed herself to be. Or had *tried* to be! Surely it had not all been false? Finding herself singing round her parents' flat, or looking up from a book to find her mother's anxious eyes upon her, she tried to resurrect old habits of concern. *Poor James*, she forced herself to think. Even though it was he who had made the break, it was she who had walked out, leaving him to clear up the mess, sell the house, put the furniture in store.

A mammoth task! Looking round the house the day that she and Muff went to pack her clothes, seeing the accumulation of several days neglect, the dust, the papers everywhere, the greasy cooker, the dirty dishes in the sink, she did feel a genuine pang. But when they had closed the last suitcase and her mother said, 'If Mrs Tomkins isn't coming, perhaps we ought to tidy up a bit, at least make the bed,' she felt anger bubble up inside her like a healing spring.

'Why should we? Why should we do anything for him? I'd have thought I'd been his bloody housemaid long enough. For Christ's sake, Muff! You said that yourself, didn't you? Or something like it.'

'All right, dear, it was just a thought,' was all her mother said, but Bridie felt her gentle tone rebuked her for vulgarity and spite.

'I don't want to stay in this house a moment longer than I have to,' she said, still angrily, then recovered herself and added, in a plaintive tone, 'I mean, of course, that I can't bear to. I'm so terribly afraid that James will turn up suddenly and start accusing us of making off with something.' She laughed sadly. 'The silver spoons. Or his mother's diamond and ruby ring.'

This was true enough. Now she had voiced this fear she *was* afraid, but her little, rueful laugh was a deliberate performance and Muff's quick, instinctive answer, 'How stupid of me, darling, I'm so sorry, we must leave *at once*,' made her shamefully aware of it.

Aware, too, that she had always orchestrated her emotions in this way to get and keep her mother's sympathy; softening down the discord of her coarser feelings and playing up the tender sounds that pleased her mother's ear. Perhaps Muff's liking for a sweet, clear tune was what was called bringing out the best in people. But it wasn't bringing out the best in her, Bridie began to feel. Only something that, although not altogether false, was never quite the truth.

James wrote to say he had 'informed the children.' A short letter, typed on his firm's headed notepaper. Since Bridie had 'clearly abdicated all responsibility,' it seemed his 'painful duty.'

Martin had left for his consulting rooms when the post arrived, and Bridie showed the letter to her mother. She said, 'The pompous ass! I wonder if he dictated this to his secretary and filed a copy. It would be like him!' She saw by the expression on her mother's face that cheerful indignation was the wrong note to strike and qualified it with a sigh. 'Poor Pansy! I've been so worried, trying to think how best to tell her, how to make it easier. I never dreamed James would do something like this without consulting me. There wasn't any *hurry* after all. I didn't think he'd be so callous.' But, secretly, she was grateful he had done it. It was true that she had worried, lying awake at night pondering how and when to break the news to Pansy, but what had occupied her, increasingly, had been embarrassment. It was somehow more humiliating to be innocent in this kind of situation than to be guilty; more shameful to be sinned-against than sinning. Easier to say, 'What a heel I am!' than 'Look how badly I've been treated.' James would enjoy striking a nobly humble stance, taking the blame upon himself . . .

As it seemed he had done. Aimee rang and wept. Tears made her pretty, deb's voice husky. 'Bridie, *duckie*, I don't know what to say! It seems so awful. So awful to do this to you. So cruel, and, you know, really horrible. I really am so awfully, frightfully sorry. I mean, if Dickie did this to me, I really think I'd want to *die*. I really think I don't want to see Daddy. I mean, you know, not ever! Dickie says that's silly. He says, even though Daddy insists it's all his fault, we don't know the whole story, and, after all, he *is* my father! I told him, you're my *mother*! I mean, that's what you are to *me*! We almost quarrelled over it, this morning when the letter came. But of course Dickie had to go and catch his train. I don't know, Bridie. I feel so miserable, and, you know, *muddled* over it. Perhaps it's being pregnant. But if you don't want me to see him Bridie, then I *won't*. Whatever Dickie says.'

'Of course you must see your father, darling,' Bridie said. 'Dickie is quite right. James would only be annoyed, and there's no point in annoying him.'

No point, either, in mentioning the allowance James gave his married daughter that paid a large chunk of the mortgage on the pretty house in Brighton from which Dickie commuted daily to his firm of diamond merchants in the city. That had been in Dickie's mind, no doubt. Even, perhaps, in Aimee's too. Her voice became at once more cheerful. 'Well, if you really don't *mind*, Bridie. I suppose it would really be most frightfully difficult, particularly with the baby coming. His first grandchild and all that. I mean, you know, he'll want to see it and I don't see how I could actually stop him coming to the hospital.'

'Of course not,' Bridie said.

'Though whether he'll *want* to come . . .' Aimee laughed – uncomfortably, it seemed. 'You know what he *is*, so busy, always. I just hope it won't be awkward.'

'Awkward?'

'Well, *you* know. . . .' Aimee said, and sighed.

'You mean it might be awkward if I came to the hospital to see you and the baby and bumped into Daddy?'

'Mmmm. . . . I suppose so. . . .' A longer sigh. Bridie smiled, and waited. Aimee said at last, 'Of course I'd rather see you, *naturally*. You know that, don't you, Bridie? Only perhaps it might be best if you checked with Dickie *first*, just to see the coast is clear.'

Bridie wondered where she would come in Dickie's pecking order of family visitors. After James, clearly. After Dickie's mother, though perhaps before his father. Dickie's parents were divorced and his father, who had a new, young wife and two small sons, was unlikely to be much help financially. Dickie's mother, on the other hand, had inherited money from her family who owned a chain of liquor stores. Even if she had not been particularly generous to Dickie up to now (James had often complained that she had 'done nothing' for the children when they married) there was the future to be thought of!

Bridie said, 'Don't worry, pet. I'll wait to hear from Dickie, I promise you! But I thought the baby wasn't due quite yet.'

'No. But it could be early, so the doctor says. That's why – I mean, *otherwise*, I'd have come to see you straightaway. With Dickie on the train this morning! But Dickie thought it would be silly, really. And besides I really do feel frightful. So fat, and, you know, *awful*!'

'Poor darling,' Bridie said.

'Oh, Bridie!' Another sigh. A catch in the voice. 'Bridie, I do miss you. I just hate to think – I mean, you won't *give me up* now, will you? I mean, because of this. I do love you. You'll come and see me sometime, won't you?'

'Of course, my love.'

Bridie put down the telephone. 'Well,' she said aloud, 'at least you know where you stand *there*!' Her voice expressed more humour than she felt. She had not expected to be put in her place so firmly, quite so soon! She didn't blame Aimee (of course not!) but she had a small, aching sense of loss. Resentment, too, though that was harder to admit. Harder because more shameful, more shameful because more selfish. All parents have to give up their children; it is the natural ending to that kind of love affair. But this wasn't the cause of her resentment. She made herself face up to it. She was resentful because now she had left James she was not, in Dickie's eyes, someone to be considered. Not Aimee's mother, not even (for much longer, anyway) Aimee's father's wife! She thought what Muff might say – 'After all you've done for that girl!' – and was shocked to find that this stereotyped phrase echoed what she felt exactly. Oh, that was petty. She would not entertain such pettiness! Sitting in her father's study, at her father's desk, she put her clenched fists to her head and groaned. Then laughed and said, 'If only I were filthy rich! Or a Duke's daughter! That would fix young Dickie!'

Adrian turned up on his motor bike. Stumping into the flat, a menacing figure in black leather; his father's golden eyes gleaming through the fair, fluffy thicket of his hair and beard. 'Oh!' he said. 'Oh, that fucking man! Jesus, Muff, I beg your pardon. Bloody hell, though. But I can't say I'm really *sorry*. I mean, Christ, Bridie, you're well out of it. It was time you split. In my opinion, honestly.'

What could be seen of his sweet, bony face, flushed red. He grabbed Bridie and hugged her fiercely. He smelled of unwashed clothes; his beard tickled her cheek. Bridie put her arms around him and felt his fragile skeleton, she said, 'Muff, darling, can we feed this hungry boy?'

'I'm not hungry,' Adrian said, releasing her. Muff went to the kitchen. He sat down on the sofa, stretching his long legs in front of him. He said, 'I mean that, Bridie, about your being lucky to be out of it. I'm sorry I swore in front of Muff. But, honestly, it never was your scene. That suburban, bourgeois encampment. England, before we lost the Empire. Like before the *Flood*! Burglar alarms and tennis clubs and coffee mornings. Not to mention Him! Jesus, Bridie, do you know what he wrote to me? *Your stepmother and I have decided to separate*! God All-Bloody-Mighty! That solemn, cold, old fish. You know, you're more my age, really.' He flushed again. 'I often used to think of that. I used to be so bloody jealous.'

'Oh, darling!' Bridie said.

'Don't pretend you didn't know it. Why else d'you think I stopped coming down to Westbridge?'

'Oh, come *on*!'

'Well; it was partly that.' He grinned at her, at ease with this situation, suddenly. '*He* didn't encourage me, exactly. Get a job, get your hair cut, and all that. But it was seeing you together I really couldn't stand. Made my flesh creep. *Yuk*!' He challenged her. 'You did know, didn't you?'

Bridie sighed.

He said, 'You stopped kissing me good night. When I was about fifteen.'

'Did I?' Bridie laughed self-consciously. He had been so beautiful. A frail, gentle, beautiful boy. She had longed to touch him, comb her fingers through his tangled, silky hair. She had thought her restraint was respect for his shy, adolescent dignity. The natural delicacy any woman would feel towards a growing son.

He said, 'It's not a guilty secret. Not as if you were my *mother*!

And you needn't look so anxious. I shan't leap on you with lust-ful cries now things are different. I mean, that's over now.'

'Oh!'

He giggled. 'Sorry, Bridie. That sounded bloody rude. I didn't mean I didn't fancy you. You know, you're very dishy, still. I only meant . . .'

She cut in, equably, 'That you've grown out of it. Grown up. I'm glad.' Bravely, she sat beside him on the sofa, took his hand, patted it, and put it back upon his knee.

He watched her thoughtfully. She felt her colour rise and was grateful when Muff entered, bringing a plate of fried eggs and toast. Both women watched him eat, in tearing, wolfish mouth-fuls. When he had finished, he lit a cigarette, inhaled, and then coughed violently. He said, 'Sorry,' sprang up, and ran to the bathroom. They heard him retching; the toilet flushed, the water ran. He came back, a fresh cigarette between his fingers, and picked up his helmet. 'Sorry about that. Well.' He assumed a cockney accent. 'Well, I suppose I'm ready for the off. Thanks, Muff. I mean, really, thanks a *lot*. I'm just not used to such delicious nosh. My eye is bigger than my stomach, as they say,' He looked at Bridie, frowning. 'If there's anything I can do. You know? I mean, I can't think what. But still.'

'I'll ask,' she said. 'I really will.'

When he had gone, Muff said, 'That's a good, dear boy in spite of everything. He'll find his feet one day. But he doesn't look after himself, does he? That cough! And he clearly doesn't eat enough.'

'Doesn't wash, either,' Bridie said.

'Dearest, that really isn't so important, is it? Not beside his health.'

'Less painful, though, to fret about his smelly feet and arm-pits than his death from malnutrition, don't you think?'

Although, in her mind's eye, Bridie immediately saw her step-son lying in an attic, pale and dead, she smiled brightly at her mother. If Muff knew how much she worried over Adrian she would be indignant with him for causing her anxiety and

Bridie could not bear to hear him criticised, even in a kindly way. She yawned and stretched elaborately to put her mother further off the scent and said, 'Actually, Muff, he's very tough. Skin and bone, but the constitution of an ox.'

Pansy's letter came the following morning.

'Dear Mother,

I was sorry to hear from Father that you had left each other. Naturally I am upset about it but I expect I'll soon get used to it. It is quite common at my school. In fact there are not many girls in my dormitory – it is in the dorm at night that we have time to find out these things – who still have their original parents. They all say there are quite a lot of advantages for children in a divorce. What they mean is, extra pocket money and holidays and presents. I am afraid this sounds materialistic but the minds of people of my age tend to linger on such things.

I had half arranged to go to Dorset at half term with Janet Morris. She is a fat girl but quite nice who is interested in Roman Britain and there is an earthworks called Maiden Castle near her house. The trouble is that Father says I must go home then and sort out my belongings because he has to sell the house and put all the things in store. Poor Father! He has so much to do! It seems a pity that you can't be there to help him. Janet Morris says it would have been much better if you had stayed in the house as he wanted you to do. She says it's a known fact that middle-aged women who have been divorced or widowed should not make sudden changes or decisions. It's bad for them psychologically. But I expect that you know best. I hope that you will be all right and that it will all work out for your future happiness. Give my love to Muff and Grandpa and tell them that I hope I shall be able to see them in the Christmas holidays if I am anywhere near London. I don't know where I am going to be, do I? I would appreciate it if you or Father would tell me what you have decided about that. And I would like to know about half term. There are not many things I want from home except my Bear. It may seem childish but I am fond of him even though he's old and his stuffing is coming out. I would like to have him with me as a reminder of the happy days that are no more.

    Peace and love,
      Pansy.

Martin said, 'Cold little cat. Takes after old James, doesn't she?'

'Really, Dadda!' Bridie, who had simply been amused and touched by Pansy's letter, by her child's attempt to be grown up, felt irritation rising. 'Pansy is just herself! I don't see why she should *take after* anyone!'

'Well, you're not cold,' her father said – as if this was sufficient answer.

'I don't know,' Bridie said impatiently. 'I don't know what I am, do I?'

She saw that this was true. If this was how people were defined, by this kind of reference – she has her mother's temperament, her father's ears! – then she had no way to define herself.

The pretty, stuffy flat was full of photographs; of Martin Mudd's brothers and sisters, grimly lined up before their terrace house in Wales and glowering at the camera; of Muff as a baby in starched christening robes, as a dreamy, flowery girl, and later, on her wedding day; of Muff's parents' wedding; of Muff's father in his clergyman's dog collar; of her dead brother who had been a pilot in the First World War, in his Air Force uniform; of her Aunt Maud, her mother's spinster sister, who had bred dogs in Shropshire. Muff had loved this aunt with whom she had spent happy summer holidays, walking dogs, gathering blueberries and blackberries and mushrooms and making apple jelly with the fruit from her orchard, and who had left her, when she died, everything she owned. The pictures of

Aunt Maud at various stages in her life, with dogs and without, showed that Muff had inherited her features as well as her small income in gilt-edged securities, her cottage and her furniture. A studio portrait of her, taken at seventy, had always stood upon Muff's dressing-table. Not only an affectionate reminder, Bridie thought, but a map, a blueprint for the future. Looking at it, in her still pretty middle age, Muff must have known exactly how her own face would pouch and sag as she grew old.

Had it been a comfort, Bridie wondered. She had no way of knowing. All the evidence of family with which her parents were surrounded was no use to her. Like the ugly duckling in the fairy tale she had no clue to what she was, or what she might become.

She had not felt she needed such a clue before. Nor did she need one now, she sternly told herself. She was a grown woman, not an adolescent girl. It was just that her life had gone wrong and she was casting round for some way to account for it, some circumstance to blame. *I am not like my mother, not her proper daughter, so of course my marriage failed*! Oh, that was too trite, too easy! Life had been too easy for her altogether; as Mary Mudd, her parents' cherished, adopted child, as Bridie Starr, a rich man's indulged young wife. That was the way to look at it! Now she must learn to stand on her own feet (as she formed this phrase she was aware that it was not quite what she meant, that she had taken it off the peg like a hastily chosen, ready-made dress) but it was close enough; a useful spur to action. And it was a sentiment that would be understood by Muff who might be hurt if she went deeper into what she felt. There was no obligation to search for hurtful aspects of the truth when there were others that would serve as well. No need to say, *I can't stay here, I cannot breathe, am stifled by your goodness, by your example that I am not equipped to follow*, though she was uncomfortably conscious that this, or something very near to it, was what she felt, increasingly. Feeling, when she was with her mother, trying to be Muff's 'tender, generous girl,' much as she felt at night in the small spare room that was so crowded with the furniture her parents had been unwilling to dispose of when they left their house after Muff's heart attack last year that there was barely room to stand beside the bed. *I am walled-up, walled-in, no room to stretch, to grow*! Less painful, and just as true, to say, 'I must think of Pansy. Make a home for her.'

She found somewhere to live. Only for six months, a temporary refuge, like her mother's clichés, but it would 'give her time to look around,' she told herself, 'a breathing space.'

One of her father's patients owned a terrace house in Islington, letting the lower floors and living on the top floor and the attic, alone except for her elderly cat. This cat, a neutered tom called Balthazar, was why Miss Lacey offered her home to Bridie: she was going to America to visit her married sister and needed someone she could trust to care for him. She trusted Bridie because she was her father's daughter; she also wanted to please Martin, as psychiatrist's patients often do.

Martin had retired from his Health Service consultancy on his seventieth birthday two years ago and most of his private practice consisted of rich Arabs who flocked from the Gulf to Harley Street like white-winged, fluttering birds, but he had kept a few old patients from his hospital clinic for whom he felt some pity, or affection, and charged them nominal fees. Miss Lacey was 'just mildly nutty', he told Bridie – speaking to his family he always used these casual, layman's terms. 'All' that was wrong with her was a belief that she was surrounded by 'spirits from the other side.' She didn't mind these spirits when they spoke to her, as they mostly did, in gentle voices; only when they attempted to be 'intimate' with her, which caused her pain. A sexual problem, otherwise she was 'pretty normal,' Martin said. Quite able, as long as she came for regular injections, to take care of herself and her old cat. Although the flat, he warned his daughter, 'might not be very clean.'

Bridie met Miss Lacey in Martin's consulting rooms to be given keys and instructions about Balthazar. She was a round-bodied little woman with a placid, pale, anonymous face,

wearing a brown coat, brown, cloche hat, brown stockings.
Her soft, fluting, genteel voice sounded only slightly nervous.
She would be at the flat when Bridie came, she said, fixing the
time, an hour before the taxi was booked to take her to the airport, but when Bridie arrived and rang the bell, there was no
answer. She realised she had expected this; let herself in,
climbed the narrow, shabby stairs – and felt as if she had come
upon the *Marie Celeste*. Miss Lacey had fled, leaving her breakfast things on the table, an egg half-eaten, coffee still warm in
the metal percolator; her bed unmade, her underclothes soak-
ing in the bathroom basin. There were signs of a last minute,
panicky attempt to clean: a tin of scouring powder and a filthy
rag beside the bath; a Hoover, flex unwound, abandoned in the
middle of the bedroom floor; in the kitchen, a plastic bin full of
rubbish, papers, empty tins of soup and cat food, mouldy hunks
of bread. On a calendar behind the kitchen door, today's date
was ringed in scarlet; the only other entries for the nine months
of this year the times of Miss Lacey's Harley Street appointments and, every four weeks, again in scarlet, in large capitals,
the one word, BLEED.

Bridie bought disinfectant, detergent, dusters, polish; took
down the curtains, washed the carpets, opened windows,
scrubbed the paint, the greasy stove. It was very hot, early
October and the last spurt of the summer's heat; in spite of it,
she worked obsessionally, enjoying the sweating exhaustion of
her body, the aching of her muscles, the savage hunger that
came on her at intervals and that she satisfied with ham rolls
and apples from the corner shop, eating them standing up,
swallowing down great lumps of fruit and bread. Occasionally,
when she was too tired and hot to work, she wept, deliberately
and noisily and rhythmically, crouching on her knees and
keening, rocking backwards and forwards. This theatrical
weeping was a pleasure she had never known before, she
thought – thinking this quite calmly while her body writhed
and moaned; this madwoman's apartment the first place
in her whole life where she had been quite alone; the

first time she had been free, no one to watch or hear.

It took four days to clean the flat. Once the dust and dirt was gone it appeared pleasant, if shabby; a bedroom and a living-room, a bathroom and a kitchen on the lower floor, and, in the attic, a large, light studio with a divan bed and a balcony that looked over a canal. From the window at night, the view was beautiful: the mysterious, dark canal below and, in the distance, tower blocks lit like fairy castles dwarfing the spires of city churches and the squat dome of St. Paul's. Bridie settled in the studio, leaving the rooms below to Balthazar who, except when she put out his food or pushed him through the studio window onto the balcony, lay mournfully growling on his mistress's bed. On the fifth morning she woke to find him on her chest, rustily purring, regarding her with an unwinking, orange stare.

'Hallo, old fool? Come to make friends, have you?' she said, and her voice sounded strange to her, cracked and unused. She realised that since she had been here, except for her shopping expeditions and a couple of telephone calls to Muff, made from the pay phone in the downstairs hall, she had spoken to no one. She had seen the other tenants in the house: a middle-aged woman with her hair piled in an old-fashioned, blonde beehive who wore short, tight skirts and shoes with high stiletto heels, and a wheezing old man who lived in the basement. But when she had smiled at them, tentatively, they had nodded and looked away.

She pushed the cat off her chest, speaking to him gently. 'All right, old fellow, I'm not rejecting you, don't worry, just let me up now and we'll see about some lovely breakfast, milk for you, coffee and toast and perhaps an egg for me. No work today, all done, we'll keep each other company.'

Balthazar purred, rubbed silkily against her naked legs, then padded down the stairs before her to the kitchen. She poured milk into his saucer, put coffee on the stove and stood at the window while it percolated, looking down at the canal, at the heavy, dusty trees that were just beginning to change colour, at a flotilla of bright, paddling ducks, at a long, painted boat that chugged slowly by, rippling the brown water. Along a path, beneath the trees on the far bank, people were exercising dogs; women in summer dresses, men in shirt sleeves, walking slowly in the shimmering morning that promised yet another unseasonably warm day. Watching them, Bridie felt her own life slow down to walking pace. The day stretched emptily ahead. Things she could do, *ought* to do – ring Muff, ring Aimee, write to Pansy – but nothing she *had* to do. She yawned and stretched, scratched an itch on her left buttock. Across the canal, a large brown and white dog with a long, feathery tale, squatted to defaecate; its owner, a tall, youngish man in jeans, stood and waited; then, glancing up at Bridie's window, grinned and waved.

She stepped back self-consciously, hugging her arms over her breasts. It seemed that there had been something casually familiar about the wave, the grin; as if he were used to looking up at this time in the morning and seeing a woman in a nightdress at this window. Was this where Miss Lacey always stood while she waited for her coffee? Bridie laughed. Surely, even at this distance, across the canal and three floors up, she looked different from Miss Lacey? Well. Perhaps not to this young man. Stopping where his dog was accustomed to relieve itself, and looking up, he simply saw what he was accustomed to see. Not Bridie Starr, a pretty, energetic woman in her early thirties, passing an idle moment watching the world go by, but poor, dotty Miss Lacey whose whole life was spent watching and waiting. Talking to her cat, listening to her spirits, waiting for her uterus to bleed . . .

Bridie laughed again, but she was shocked. And frightened. She ran into the bathroom and looked into the glass front of Miss Lacey's medicine cabinet. Her face looked back at her: wild, dark eyes beneath wildly curling, uncombed hair. A startled, guilty face – much madder than Miss Lacey's.

She spoke to this mad face, said, spitefully, 'How do you know you won't go mad, my girl? You've no idea what lies in wait for you!'

Chapter Three

She dreamed that James was dead. Waking, she remembered no details of her dream, only that he had in some way committed suicide. She was interested to find that her first reaction was relief – no more to fear from him, no more needling letters, no need, now, to bother with solicitors, settlements, divorce . . .

How callous she had become, she thought, attempting to reproach herself but in fact she didn't really care; it seemed that when she left Westbridge she had left behind her finer feelings along with her role of mother, wife and housekeeper. That she could change so easily bewildered her; she was a little nervous of the cold, uncaring, self-preserving woman she felt she had become.

The coldness was only temporary, she told herself. She was in a state of shock. Perhaps Pansy had been right: she should not have left her home so suddenly. Like a refugee she had lost her roots, her sense of place.

Exploring the streets and squares round the canal this sense of displacement grew. Some of the graceful terrace houses, built a hundred years ago for up-and-coming city clerks, had recently been bought and renovated by young professional couples who could not afford Chelsea or Kensington. Green

bay trees in ornamental pots stood outside the freshly painted
doors and, through picture windows fitted in the damp old
basements modern kitchens could be seen; dishwashers, steel
sinks, blenders, stripped pine furniture. Of the houses that had
not been rescued – 'gentrified' was the local jargon – many were
quite derelict, doors and windows boarded up with corrugated
iron, but in others people still seemed to be living, tending
woody geraniums in leaky window-boxes, putting out plastic
bags of garbage on the crumbling steps.

Avoiding these garbage bags that often spilled their stinking
contents on the pot-holed pavements, picking her way through
piles of dog shit (since Irish wolf hounds were fashionable
among the young professional couples some of these droppings
were enormous) it seemed to Bridie that her old life had been
lived not only in another country but in another planet; light
years, millennia, away. It was hard to believe that the same sun
shone down on the watered golf courses, the swimming-pools
and private zoos of Westbridge Hill as on the urban desolation
that surrounded her. To her despairing mind (she was beginning to recognise her coldness as despair) the brave attempts to
improve this area of the inner city, the small municipal gardens,
the adventure playgrounds for the children, the litter bins and
seats alongside the canal, merely pointed up the squalor. The
benches were occupied by sprawling drunks who filled the litter
bins with bottles; the newly planted trees were caged with wire
against the vandals; the children ignored the playgrounds, pre-
ferring to fish for treasure beneath the detergent foam that
streaked the brown canal, or smashing the windows of the
huge, empty, looted factories and warehouses that lined the
banks downstream, below the lock, like monuments in a mu-
seum of industrial archaeology.

Like the buildings, most of the people Bridie saw when she was
walking in the mornings seemed abandoned; soiled or damaged
in some way. The owners of the renovated houses departed
after breakfast in their Volkswagen and Volvo cars, the children
went to school, leaving the streets and the canal walkways to

shabby housewives, winos, the unemployed, the crippled; the detritus of the city washed up here like the dead cats, the plastic bottles and the rotten fruit that bobbed against the closed gates of the lock. Bridie thought she had never seen a place where the melancholy aspects of life were so exaggerated. The tramps were filthier, the drunkards drunker. The homosexual who lived in the house opposite was a mincing parody; long, curled hair in ribbons, one dangling gold ear-ring, tiny, teetering feet in high-heeled shoes; the Cypriot who ran the corner shop had one eye and a wooden peg-leg instead of a proper artificial limb; the lonely and the mad gesticulated, laughed or wept or talked – but only to themselves, avoiding each other's eyes. If Bridie smiled at someone she was passing, they almost always looked away.

One morning, an old woman did speak to her; sat down beside her on a bench by the canal and said, 'You don't mind if I rest me feet a bit?'

'Of course not.' Bridie moved along the bench. 'Isn't it a lovely day?'

The old woman gave a tired and rustling sigh. Her swollen little feet, in carpet slippers, swung clear of the ground. 'I don't get out much,' she said, 'but you have to make the effort, don't you?'

Bridie said, 'On a day like this it's worth it.' She spoke in an encouraging, bright voice and the woman looked at her briefly and suspiciously; pale eyes in a pale, papery old face.

'All right, I suppose,' she admitted somewhat grudgingly. 'Down here by the water. Up where I live, the ninth floor of them flats, it's been an oven all this summer. They ought to pay us for living there, I reckon. Lifts out of order half the time, bloody kids sitting on the stairs and sniffing glue. Catch them at it, they don't care! I mean, you'd be a fool to call the police round here. It's not safe to complain, they'd only get you for it. It's worst in the evenings. You sit, listening to them racketing up and down and think what they could do. I never go outside my door at night now. I used to go to Bingo when my husband was alive but since he passed on I don't seem to have the heart no more.'

'I'm sorry,' Bridie said.

'A bit of myself went with him. Even though you couldn't have wished anything else, really. He'd gone away to nothing the last months. Big, hefty man, six foot, but he went down to five stone before the end. Skin and bone and no joy anymore except for a bit of a drink down the pub Saturdays. I never go now. Don't go anywhere. No point in it. I mean, one place is like another, isn't it? When you're alone. That's what I tell my boys.'

'You've got children, then?' Bridie said, seizing on what might turn out to be a happier topic.

The woman nodded. 'They're good boys, don't you think otherwise! Five of them, all grown and married and they all think the world of me. If I wanted anything, I'd only have to say the word. Not that I'd say it, mind. Taking from your children always changes things. I mean, you've looked after them. Course I go to see them but never more than just the day. Nothing like your own bed and I wouldn't impose, anyway, I've seen too much of that. I've got a neighbour, Peggy, she comes in, sees I'm all right, runs down to the shop for me when my legs are bad. They started to go after my husband died; some mornings it's like moving lumps of lead. Peggy gets me my paper and my cigarettes and a bit of something for my dinner. I think one of my sons slips her something now and then. I hope he does, in a way, though it's nice to think she wouldn't take it.'

'Oh, I know *exactly* what you mean!' Although as soon as she had spoken, Bridie feared she sounded condescending, she was glad to find something she could respond to in this gloomy monologue.

'I'd never ask her naturally. But I've noticed she likes to pop in when my boys come to see me. Soon as one of them comes, she's knocking at my door with some excuse. I get a bit narked sometimes but then I think, well, she's got no one of her own.

She had a baby during the war, you know, but it wasn't her husband's. He was in the Army and when he came home and found her with the baby he wouldn't let her keep it. A few months old, still at the breast! He just came in one night with papers for her to sign, adoption papers, and took it away the next day. He died a twelve month later, the husband, and she couldn't find out what happened to the baby. She's fifty now and she still thinks about it, she says it gets worse, not better. There's this new law come out, children who've been adopted can look up their parents if they want to. Nothing about parents finding out about their kids, though. I think that's worse. Peggy showed me all about this new law in the papers, crying and carrying on. It brought it up fresh to her, you see, all that she'd lost, and now she broods about it all the time. It's partly her age, of course. I try and cheer her up. I tell her, I've got five good children and I'm grateful for them but they can't make up for him that's gone. No child can take a husband's place. That's what I tell Peggy when she's down.'

'Not much comfort if she's lost her husband, too,' Bridie murmured. She had written to Pansy, *There are a lot of fascinating old characters round here*, but, really, she was repelled by them, not fascinated. This sad old woman with her rambling tongue and lumpy feet hardly seemed human to her. Shocked by this thought, she said quickly, 'What a dreadful story! Was it a girl or a boy? Peggy's baby?'

'Oh, I don't know, love. She's never said and I never liked to ask. You don't like to rub the salt in, do you?'

Aimee's son was born. The birth was easy, Dickie said, when Bridie telephoned. Aimee was 'in cracking form' and they were 'all' delighted with the baby. He was, Dickie said, 'a tremendously jolly little chap.'

Although Bridie had heard Dickie talk like this before it seemed now that this effusive, bar room heartiness was put on to cloak embarrassment. Obviously they had 'all' – Dickie's parents, James – already seen the baby. Equally obviously,

Dickie didn't want her there; a wicked, absconding step-mother, breathing over his son's cot like a bad fairy! All right, then! If she wasn't asked, she wouldn't ask to come! Leaning against the wall beside the telephone, she was seized with trembling rage, like a sudden, violent illness.

She closed her eyes; breathed deeply. She said, 'I'm so glad, Dickie. Will you give my love to Aimee?'

'Surely,' Dickie said. 'Of course I will.' He hesitated, then laughed in a surprised way.

Bridie said smoothly, 'Tell her that I'm longing to see her and the baby but I'll wait until she's out of hospital. I expect she's got enough visitors at the moment, hasn't she?'

'Well,' Dickie said. He laughed again, awkwardly.

'All those devoted grandparents!' Bridie assumed a playful tone. 'Who does he take after?'

'Oh, I don't know. Honestly, Bridie. A little, bald old man. Aimee says he looks a bit like me but I'm not sure that's a compliment.'

'Have you decided what to call him yet?'

'Richard, probably. Richard Merlin is what Aimee wants. I thought, Richard James.'

'Very sensible,' Bridie said. She thought – That ought to put the allowance up a bit! A picture of Dickie rose up before her; a handsome, square-faced young man with a hard, square mouth like a money-box. Poor baby, if he really did look like his father! She said. 'No mileage in calling him after a dead magician, is there?'

Dickie was silent for several seconds. Then he said, 'It was just a little fanciful, I thought. The kind of name a boy might find embarrassing at school.'

'Oh,' Bridie said. 'Yes. Yes, I see. I expect you're right.'

Another pause. Dickie said, 'I'll give your love to Aimee, then?'

'If you would. Please.'

He said, 'You know, Bridie, she really is so *fond* of you.'

It wasn't until she put the telephone down that she

understood this was meant as a reproach. Dickie had expected her to ask for a time when she could visit the hospital and, when she didn't, had been hurt on Aimee's behalf. Rightly, Bridie thought. Oh, how ridiculous! A silly misunderstanding. How stupid she had been, vindictive, spiteful, thinking only of herself, of how *she* had been rejected, pushed aside by Dickie because she wasn't Aimee's 'proper' mother – all her love and care disregarded! – while *he* had been nervous of presuming on her affection for precisely that same reason!

But she still felt resentful; a dark, unreasoning anger swelling up inside her like a tumour, rising in her throat and choking her.

She felt she couldn't breathe. She went out of the house, walking aimlessly and quickly, almost running, muttering under her breath, composing speeches. She should have spoken calmly to Dickie, made her attitude clear to him. 'I love Aimee as if she were my own. In fact, in a real sense, she *is*. I brought her up since she was six years old. That's what matters, isn't it? The blood tie is so unimportant, so crude and primitive.'

It was nine o'clock in the evening. Windows were open onto the warm night. She slowed down and looked into lit ground floor rooms, into basement kitchens. People sat and talked, cooked, washed the dishes; families laughing and quarrelling. Only she was shut out, talking to herself like one of the city's mad vagabonds, lonely and wandering. That was nonsense, of course! She wasn't shut out. All she had to do was to get on a bus, hail a taxi, cross London to Eaton Square, ring her parents' bell. They would understand her hurt, soothe it, bandage her wound which, although it felt so deep and painful, was really trivial. Self-inflicted, too! Dickie had not meant to slight her; it was she who had been over-sensitive, absurdly edgy! Not that she should blame herself for it! As Muff might say, 'No one is perfect.' She laughed out loud and an approaching couple, a middle-aged man and woman, looked at her curiously. She said, 'Good evening,' speaking clearly and pleasantly, but they didn't answer and she thought they quickened their pace as they passed her.

She came to the main road. Cabs, cars, huge cumbersome trucks, swaying buses, swept past her, stirring up eddies of dust and rags of old newspaper that wrapped round her ankles. She stopped at the next side street where there was a telephone booth on one corner and a public house on the other that was noisily cheerful; doors open, men standing on the pavement, drinking and smoking.

She went into the telephone booth, thinking that she might ring Dickie, apologise for her curtness, ask if she might visit Aimee tomorrow, but the floor of the booth was dark with dried urine and the instrument smashed, the broken receiver dangling at the end of its cord. On the wall someone had written, FUCK ALL POOFS, and below, a more elegant hand had inscribed a subtler message. *The Meek don't want it!*

This made her smile. She came out of the booth, smiling, and a man called from the public house, from the opposite pavement. 'Hallo, my lovely. Have a beer, how about it?' A slurred but friendly voice; a stocky man in a white shirt. She waved her hand, acknowledging his invitation, shaking her head, still smiling gaily.

She walked down the side street. On one side a row of houses were being demolished; skips, full of rubble and festooned with warning lanterns, stood in the roadway. On the other, iron railings fenced off a concrete playground; the school buildings beyond it were dark. She was halfway down this quiet street, walking alongside the empty playground, when feet came running behind her. She turned and two men were upon her, thrusting her against the railings. A hand covered her mouth; another hand thrust up her skirt, scrabbling and tugging. 'Come on,' one of them said, 'you asked for it, didn't you?' She wrenched her mouth free, tried to scream, but was slammed back, breathless, against the railings. One man was holding her, twisting her arms back, and his heavy boot, thumping down on her foot, hurt her more than the other man's fingers jabbing inside her. 'Dry as a bloody bone,' this man said, and punched the side of her face. They let her go and she slid down the railings, one leg doubled beneath her. She stayed like this, trembling, while they ran off down the road and disappeared round the corner. Waiting for someone to come, help her up, dust her down, call the police . . .

No one came. Several men, including the man in the white shirt who had offered her beer, were watching from the public house a few hundred yards away; as she picked herself up, one of them laughed. Only with relief, perhaps, but she felt outraged – how could they *stand* there, seeing an innocent woman half-raped in front of their eyes? – then, humiliated. She wasn't an innocent woman to them! She had smiled and waved; a tart, 'asking for it.' She found her bag in the gutter and limped off down the street, the way her attackers had gone. Suppose they were waiting round the next corner? Don't be a fool, she told herself sternly; they had run off, a couple of stupid drunks, one brutal impulse – they hadn't even stolen her purse! Fighting the panic, the fear that made her head swim, she came to the end of the street and saw the dark canal straight ahead of her and another public house, throwing golden light on the pavement; light, comfort and safety . . .

This was a quiet, well-kept pub; a few men, a couple of women, no juke-box playing. She went to the bar and asked for a whisky. The man glanced at her; then away. He filled her glass, took the pound note she proffered and handed her change, without raising his eyes to her face. She sat on a stool and sipped at her drink. Beside her, an elderly man asked for beer. He looked gentle and respectable. She thought, I could tell him what happened! She caught his eye and gave a small, rueful smile. He responded, but briefly and nervously, and took his beer back to his table. She looked round but everyone was sitting silent and staring in front of them. Zombies, she thought. She turned on her stool and saw her face in the glass behind the bottles at the back of the bar. It was white, streaked with dirt, a bruise coming up on one cheek. Her dress was filthy, too. Of course they all shrank from her! She looked like a derelict who had fallen down drunk in the street, a pariah. I am nothing, she thought, I am nobody. I have no father, no mother, no husband, no lover. She smiled at her nothing-face, brightly and bravely, and finished her whisky.

The bruise developed overnight. In the morning it was yellow and brown and blue. The eye above it was slightly puffy with a red blob of blood in one corner. Blood on her skirt, too – she must have started to menstruate after the men had attacked her. She put the dress to soak in cold water and cooled her cheek with witch hazel. When she went out to buy tinned cat meat for Balthazar, no one she saw in the street or the shop gave her more than a casual glance. Perhaps black eyes and bruises were common round here, or perhaps the bruise was not as bad as she'd thought. But when she got back to the flat, it seemed worse; a bright, tight, shiny swelling that made the rest of her face look hollowed and pale.

She telephoned her father's secretary in Harley Street and asked if he were likely to be free around lunch time. The girl said there was nothing in Dr. Mudd's diary; she was sure he would be pleased to see Bridie. 'Don't tell him I'm coming,' Bridie said, suddenly nervous. 'I might change my mind.'

She arrived at Martin's surgery, just before one o'clock, as an Arab family was leaving; an impressive, huge-bellied man, two women in black robes with stiff, silvery masks over their faces, and several plump, giggling children. Bridie went up in the lift to the second floor. The secretary looked up from her desk on the carpeted landing. Bridie said, 'All those Arabs!'

The girl started to grin. She saw Bridie's face and stopped. She said, uneasily, 'At least that last lot didn't need an interpreter.'

Bridie put her hand to her cheek. She said, 'I could do with one of those fancy yashmaks. I opened a door on myself. One that usually sticks but for some reason it didn't. I gave an extra hard tug and – *Wham*!' She acted this out, reeling back, gasping.

The girl said, 'It looks really painful. You should see a doctor.'

'I'm seeing one, aren't I?' Bridie said, laughing.

Her father was sitting in an old leather armchair, feet on his desk, listening to the Ninth Symphony. His eyes were closed and he was weaving one hand about, idly conducting the music. He looked tired. A tired, skinny old owl, Bridie thought. She said, 'Dadda,' and he opened his eyes, grunted, and took his feet off the desk. He glanced at her quickly, got up, and went to the record player. He turned the volume down low and said, 'Marvellous man. Unbelievable. Everything there, all human life. As far as I'm concerned, you can keep every other composer. Beethoven's enough for me in my lifetime. What have you done to your face?'

'I was mugged,' Bridie said. 'Not very seriously. Lost my bag, but there wasn't much in it.' She wondered why she couldn't tell her father the truth and, anticipating an awkward question, amplified her lie. 'Luckily I had the door keys in my pocket.'

He came up to her and touched her cheek lightly. 'It'll go down. Do you want a drink? Sherry? Or coffee? Plenty in the thermos. And your mother always makes too many sandwiches. I tell her not to bother but she makes them before she goes to bed and puts them in the tin. You can share my workingman's lunch! Unless you'd rather go out? There's an Italian place that's quite good.'

'No thank you, Dadda.'

'Good. I get a bit tired, can't digest properly this time of the day.'

'You ought to stop working, Dadda. It's time you stopped, isn't it? You can afford to, you've earned enough, surely?'

'It's not that.' He gave his sharp, barking laugh. 'I'm a glutton for work. Like my father. When he left the mine he shrivelled and died. Couldn't think what to do with himself. Florence has been feeling it, too, since she retired from her school.' He

laughed again, loudly and shortly. 'Only she's got an occupa-
tion at the moment. Stirring up trouble. Right old ding-dong
blowing up . . .' He poured sherry and returned to his armchair with his glass. He leaned back, looked at her, and said,
'Well, what have you come for?'

'Oh. Nothing. That is, it can wait.' Bridie smiled at him
brightly. 'What's up with Aunt Florence? You tell me that
first.'

'Well. You know your Aunt Blodwen?'

'The one that went to Australia?'

'Yes. In the 'twenties. In 1929, to be exact. She was eighteen
then, five years younger than Blanche, six years younger than
Florence. Blodwen was the youngest of the three girls and the
prettiest. Florence, the oldest and ugliest. She was always a bit
jealous, by nature, but Blodwen gave her real cause. All ancient
history. Nearly fifty years. . . .' He chuckled – Bridie saw this
wasn't ancient history to him. 'Put briefly, if not exactly in a
nutshell. Florence had a young man, another schoolteacher.
She brought him home and he fell for Blodwen. Worse – when
Harry and Blodwen got married, they emigrated. Blanche was
married already, living in Scotland, Sam working in the Post
Office in Cardiff, so Florence was the only one left at home to
look after Mother. Who was a domineering old bitch, as I
daresay I've told you. Florence stayed with her, nursed her
when she got ill, put up with her tantrums. Taught at the local
elementary school, became the Headmistress, but if she hadn't
been tied, been free to move to a bigger school, she'd have done
a lot better. If Blodwen had stayed in Wales, at least she could
have shared the responsibility. Florence forgave her, wrote to
her, Christmas and birthdays, but she never forgave Harry.
Never spoke of him in her letters to Blodwen though she sent
letters to her two boys, her children. As if Blodwen had had
them by Immaculate Conception, Blanche used to say. Well.
That's the background. Now Blodwen has written to say she's
coming home for six months and Florence, after a bit of old
tarra-diddle and fuss, has taken it well. But she's written back

to Blodwen saying she's looking forward to seeing them *both*. Both Blodwen and *Harry*. Breaking all those years' silence. Old Florence is decent enough when it comes to the push. Poor old Florence.'

He snorted, rolling the stem of his sherry glass in his fingers. Bridie said, 'Go on, Dadda. You said, *all this ding-dong*! But if they've made it up, there can't be much wrong. When's Blodwen coming?'

'Few weeks time. And there's a lot wrong!' He savoured this satisfaction along with his sherry; draining his glass. 'The thing is, Harry's dead. Died seven years ago. Blodwen didn't tell Florence, naturally. And the rest of us didn't think it our business to, either. No point, we all thought. After all, he'd been dead to Florence for a good many long years. His actual interment simply made it official. I suppose we should have anticipated something like this. Now there's no way round I can see. Florence is going to feel such a bloody fool! Especially since she's made the grand gesture. Welcoming Harry! That corpse! And, my God, how Blodwen will crow!'

Bridie said, 'I don't see why she should, Dadda. After all, she must have realised, when she got Florence's letter that Florence didn't know Harry was dead. I mean, until then, she might have assumed that someone – one of you – must have told her.'

'Well, she knows better now,' Martin said. 'And she'll crow because she's one up on Florence. You can see why, can't you? Blodwen will know what a struggle Florence must have had with her pride and her conscience. And all for nothing! You must admit it has it's comic side.'

He got up from his chair and opened the cupboard beside the wash-basin. He took out a thermos flask, two mugs, two plates, and an old, scratched tin box. This tin box had once belonged to his father; had held lumps of cold bacon and cheese to be eaten in the dusk and the dark, at the coal face. Now it contained smoked salmon sandwiches wrapped in Cling Film. Martin divided the sandwiches between the two plates. He said, 'Comic and sad. I suppose I'll have to tell Florence. Get round to it somehow. Too cruel to let her go to the airport, not knowing. Though Blodwen would be amused by that situation! People don't change much, and she was always a spiteful girl, your Aunt Blodwen. Took after our mother, more than the rest of us.'

Bridie's head was buzzing. She thought – Alcohol on an empty stomach. She had not eaten last night; had only had coffee this morning. She said. 'She's not *my* Aunt Blodwen!'

Her father looked at her. She put her empty sherry glass down on the desk. She said, 'Dadda, darling!'

He said, suspiciously, 'What's all this about?'

'This family saga. All this *past* behind you. It's not mine, is it? Not my family! Not in the sense that I can measure myself, see who I *take after*!'

'Lucky girl, I'd say!' Martin laughed.

'Don't fob me off, Dadda! What I mean is, of course I care about them, as I care about Muff's family, what's left of it, because I love you and Muff, nothing can ever change that. I don't need another family, not to *love*. Just to *know*! I've never felt this before. I suppose it's the break up with James. I mean, before that, I knew where I was going, what I was doing. Or thought I knew. Now that's over, I really know *nothing*. Where to go, what to do, what I'm *fitted* for. I don't want to make another mistake. And it's more than that. Worse. I feel – I don't know, sort of *shadowy*. A face and a voice, a pair of legs walking. When those two men, when they grabbed me . . .'

Tears came up, choking her. She put her hands to her face. She wailed, 'It made me feel like a nothing. A nobody.'

Martin said, 'Here, take my hanky.'

He stood over her. A clean handkerchief appeared on her lap. She took out the folds; blew her nose. She said, not looking up, 'I want to know who my parents were, Dadda. You told me I was an orphan. I suppose that's all that you know. Would you mind if I tried to find out? It's possible now. I can make an application to the Registrar General. Though it may not work in my case. So long ago, during the war, some records must have been lost or destroyed . . .' She felt giddy, suddenly. Giddy and foolish. She laughed and said, 'After all, it could be important. For God's sake, my mother might have been mad! Like Miss Lacey! Other things, too. You said, about James, that he was old enough to be my father! Well, he could have been, couldn't he?'

'You can set your mind at rest on both those points,' Martin said grimly. She gathered her courage and looked at him. Saw his cheeks flushing up; little pads, wired with red, thready veins.

She said, 'Well, they're not serious. The rest is. I really do feel it's important to me. It's all chance, perhaps. I met a woman by the canal. She was talking about this new law. Some friend of hers – oh, that doesn't matter. But it started me thinking.'

He said nothing. He turned and went back to his chair and sat down, hands on knees, looking old. A tired, thin old man; the flushed skin stretched tight over the frame of his face.

She said, 'I'm sorry, Dadda.'

He shook his head. 'Don't apologise. I suppose I should be surprised that this hasn't come up before.' He sat, watching her.

She said, 'Once, some years ago, I read an article in one of your magazines. About adopted children. How they suffer from what's called genealogical bewilderment. Like Hans Andersen's ugly duckling.'

'Bloody rubbish!'

She smiled. 'I thought you'd say that. I think I thought *rubbish* too, at the time. But I felt ashamed, reading this article, in case you or Muff came in and caught me. I remember, I stuffed the magazine back in the rack, hiding it, feeling guilty. So it must have meant something. I must have wondered, deep down. Or perhaps I'm so shallow, I didn't! Just accepted what I seemed to be on the surface. A nice girl! You and Muff made that easy.' She stopped. 'That's not a complaint. I am grateful to you and Muff, Dadda.'

He winced. 'Oh, stuff that! And call me Martin, for God's

sake. All this Muff, Dadda, business. As if you were still five years old.'

She said, stiffly, 'I'm sorry.'

'No. I don't object, really. Forget it. Look. I'm sorry I went on about my blasted family. That seems to have triggered you off as much as anything else. I don't care for them all that much now, but once we needed each other. The background I came from, you needed a family for economic survival. I had a scholarship to medical school but if Florence and Sam hadn't been working I'd have gone hungry. Everything else is just bloody whimsy.' He glared at her. 'Boredom's your trouble.'

'Would you say that if I came to you as a patient?'

'Probably. Though if I was being paid for my opinion, I daresay I'd wrap it up a bit.'

'There's Pansy. I can't get a job until after the Christmas holidays.'

'It wouldn't hurt her if you did something part time. But your business. Your daughter.'

'Yes, Dadda. *Martin*! Don't shout at me!' But his temper had stiffened her. 'Whether I have a job or not is really irrelevant. You know it is, too. So is whether I'm bored or not. The thing is, I've made my mind up. I've got a right to know.'

'Rights, rights,' he said scornfully. He got up and went to the window where he stood, shoulders hunched, staring out. 'You understand, I suppose, that it won't solve anything. You're intelligent enough to know that. And it may hurt other people. Muff, for example.'

'She needn't know.'

'Oh, she'll have to. She's the one that can tell you. No need to go chasing round record offices. Muff knew your mother. She can tell you about her. I should wait a few days until that bruise has gone down, though.'

'I can tell her I tripped and fell on the pavement. But I'd rather you told me.'

'Well, I'd rather *not*.' He turned round and looked at her, his face shadowed and gloomy.

'Ducking out, are you?'

'If you like. Various reasons . . .' His baleful tone and his sigh hinted that these might be tortuous. She thought – Oh, those devious Mudds! Making life complicated, hugging mysteries, secrets, locking cupboard doors on their rattling skeletons! He said, slightly more cheerfully, 'One is, that Muff may prefer to. Though it may break her heart, mind!'

She said, 'Rubbish, Dadda!'

Chapter Four

'I have always wanted to tell you, my darling,' Muff said. 'When you were a little girl, three or four, sitting on my lap saying, *Muff tell me a story*, I often thought, one day she'll want to know, and I'd practise how I would do it, what I would say. Telling you like a fairy tale I thought, when you were little. But Dadda said no, not if you didn't ask. I'm glad you've asked now because I think it is something you should know. Although I would never have gone against Dadda, and I understood how he felt, that he wanted you to feel you belonged to us wholly, I always felt it was wrong.'

If Muff's heart was broken, then she was a good actress! Seeing her tranquil smile, her blue eyes clear as calm pools, Birdie felt – absurdly, she recognised – a slight sense of pique. Had Muff *not* felt, then, that the little girl on her knee 'belonged to her wholly'? Had she kept some part of herself, of her love, in reserve against just this moment? So she could give her up without pain? Oh, of course not. This was the sort of argument Dadda would put up, Bridie thought; the way *his* jealous mind worked. She despised herself for it!

Muff said, 'Of course it was always easier for me than for Dadda. I loved your mother so much that I felt you were doubly precious. Not only my baby, but a gift *she* had given me.'

She stopped; turned her head. Bridie looked at her profile –

fluffy white hair, short nose, soft baggy chin – silhouetted against the light from the window. She was sitting so still, hands clasped in her lap, feet side by side on a silk-covered stool, that Birdie did not dare move or speak.

Muff said, at last, 'Darling, there's a photograph album in the top drawer of the bureau. A brown one with a brass clasp.'

Bridie felt as if she were committing a crime. She opened the drawer, feeling guilty and greedy – like a child stealing sweets. The crime was on that sort of level, she thought. The album was at the bottom of the drawer under some papers.

Muff balanced it on her knees and opened the clasp. The stiff pages fell open. 'Look,' Muff said, her voice suddenly girlish and eager, 'Look, darling. Your mother, Hermione, and me, and a friend of ours, Hetty.'

Bridie looked at a faded sepia photograph of three little girls in laced boots and pinafores. Muff said, 'Your mother is the dark one in the middle. Hetty and me either side. This was taken our first year at boarding school which was where we met. Hermione and I had beds next to each other. I remember she cried the first night, she was so cold and lonely, and I got into bed with her. I think Hetty was in another dormitory but we were all three such close friends, until poor darling Hetty died in that terrible 'flu. The Three Aitch Sisters, we called ourselves because our names all began with H. Hilary and Hermione and Hetty. And when we wrote notes to each other, we always said, O Friend of My Bosom! We shared everything, the extra things our parents sent us, biscuits and cakes. It was the First World War, you see, and the food was bad, and we were often so hungry. We used to go for walks and pick nettles for the cook to make nettle soup. I remember that the nettles stang, even through my thick woollen gloves, and I always had chilblains. Not as badly as Hetty, though. Hers used to crack and bleed and I used to pick her nettles for her because they hurt her so much. Poor Hetty was a frail little mortal . . .'

She laughed nervously. She said, 'Oh, I'm sorry, dear. I shouldn't run on like this. You don't want to hear about my chilblains, and Hetty . . .'

Bridie knelt beside her and put her arms round her. Muff kissed her cheek, then released herself gently. She said, 'Thank you, dear, but you mustn't distract me. Let me see, now. Hermione's face isn't very clear in that photograph.'

She turned the pages. A girl sat on a high stool in a stiff-skirted ballet dress, her long, pale-stockinged legs and long feet carefully pointed, a bouquet of flowers loosely held in her lap, more flowers in her dark, braided hair.

'She must have been about seventeen,' Muff said. 'She was a good dancer. So tall and so graceful.'

Bridie looked at the picture. Muff was waiting expectantly. Bridie said, 'She's quite pretty.' She felt nothing for this pretty girl.

'Oh, she was *lovely*,' Muff said. 'Pretty and clever! She should have gone to university, really, but in those days girls – girls of our sort, that is – were not expected to earn their own livings. My parents allowed me to train as a nurse but they were very unusual people. And Hermione – your mother – married so young. At nineteen. It was very romantic. She eloped with an Army lieutenant called Gilbert Lash and married him in a registry office. I don't quite know why she didn't have a proper wedding. Or perhaps I knew once, and just can't remember. She must have had her parents' permission at that age. Perhaps she just didn't want all the fuss! All I really know is that she came to the hospital where I was working the day before she got married and asked me if I would be one of her witnesses. I was on duty that night until eight in the morning so I had to go straight there in my uniform. I can remember being embarrassed, feeling I was letting Hermione down in my awful flat shoes and black stockings. And feeling so sleepy! There must have been some pictures taken but I'm afraid all I've got is one of Hermione that she sent me afterwards.'

Hermione's hair was cropped short in this picture, little spikes of hair flat to her forehead. She wore a straight, waistless dress with a hem cut in points, several long strings of beads and pointed, strap shoes. Bridie said, feeling something now, feeling cold towards this strange young woman who had embarrassed Muff, making her come straight from night duty to the registry office, wearing her uniform, 'If she was nineteen then, she was quite old when I was born, wasn't she? In 1944.'

'Thirty eight,' Muff said. 'Oh dear, yes! A lot of water had flowed under the bridge.'

'Was her husband, this Gilbert, my father?'

Muff looked astonished. 'No, of course not. I mean, if he had been . . .' She stopped, screwing up her face helplessly. Perhaps this was harder than she had expected. Bridie longed to take her hand but it seemed the wrong moment. Muff was so far away; her mind reaching back, concentrating. She closed her eyes and a little, determined line appeared on her forehead that Bridie had not seen before.

She said, 'It wasn't a happy marriage. Although of course I didn't know that for a long time. Gilbert was posted abroad. When they came home on leave we saw them occasionally, but I was married by then and Dadda didn't like Gilbert. Dadda isn't a drinking man, as you know. He likes sherry, a glass of wine with a meal, but not to settle down with a bottle of whisky which was Gilbert's idea of a night's entertainment. But it was more than that.' Muff lowered her voice. 'Gilbert was a *brutal* man. Not that he knocked your mother about. I am sure that if he had, she'd have left him. But it was something you sensed even when he was sober. As if there was a dangerous spring coiled inside him that only needed a touch, a wrong word. Not that Hermione ever complained to me, she was always loyal to him. When we were alone she was her old, cheerful self, full of fun, bright and breezy. But when Gilbert was there she was very much quieter. She watched him all the time as if she were afraid to provoke him, set off that *spring*. Of course, one never knows what goes on in a marriage but I am afraid that he bullied her.'

Bridie wondered how true this was. There was an air of rehearsal about it and a certain uneasiness. Perhaps the idea of a bullying husband was so shocking to Muff that it pained her to speak of it. But it seemed to Bridie that, for once in her life, Muff was inventing; providing an excuse for what was to come later.

Hermione had two children: a boy, nine years after her marriage, and a girl in 1937, the same year that Muff's daughter, Grace, had been born. Her children were born in Malta, where Gilbert Lash was stationed; Muff did not see them until 1939 when Hermione brought them to England at the outbreak of war.

Martin Mudd joined the Army as a medical officer and was posted to Scotland. Muff and Grace went to stay with Aunt Maud in Shropshire and, a year later, when the bombing of London began, Hermione joined them. There was not enough room in Aunt Maud's cottage for her to stay long with the children, but Muff found her a couple of rooms in a farmhouse within walking distance. 'Very simple,' Muff said, 'but clean and quite nicely furnished and with a beautiful view of the hills. Of Aunt Maud's cottage, too – if Hermione and I stood at our windows we could wave to each other! I was pleased about that because I was worried in case Hermione should be a little bit lonely. She'd never lived in the country, and Fowler's Farm was rather isolated. And although the people who owned it, the Dobsons, were friendly and welcoming, a nice man, a sweet woman, and two pretty daughters, they were all so busy working, in the fields, in the dairy. Help was hard to come by during the war and though later on they had an Italian prisoner, as a lot of the farms did, they had no one just then. So I told Hermione – if you're bored and want someone to talk to, just stand at your window and wave a red handkerchief and Grace and I will come over! It sounds childish, but in a way, dear, we both felt like girls again. No husbands – Gilbert was overseas and though Dadda came sometimes, from Scotland, he couldn't come often – no social life to arrange, no dinner parties, just ourselves and our babies. We were so carefree! We used to harness up the Dobsons' old pony trap and rattle round the quiet lanes, taking picnics up in the hills, blackberrying, picking mushrooms, all the things I used to do with Aunt Maud, when I was a little girl. Poor old thing, she was too frail to come with us and her mind was beginning to drift the way old people's minds sometimes do, but I think she liked it when the children ran in to show her the things they had gathered and I was glad, even though I missed Dadda, to think I was able to be with her, now that she ₁eeded me. It seems dreadful in a way, looking back and remembering the war was on all that time, so many terrible things happening everywhere, and yet we were as happy as larks! So happy and lucky, to have this long, calm time in our lives. Three wonderful, peaceful years in the middle of a terrible war! It was such a beautiful part of the country and everyone was so kind to us, all the farm people, and it was lovely to watch our children growing so rosy and strong in the sweet, country air. When I think of Gracie now, I see her running towards me under the chestnut trees down the lane that went to the farm, her pink little face so pleased and excited, calling out, 'Look, all those *fat* conkers!'

Although the light, joyful note went from her voice, she spoke of Gracie's death calmly. This was Hermione's story, not hers, and the little girl's brief, terrible illness was only an episode in it. Muff had refused to let Hermione come near her in case she should carry infection to her own children, and afterwards, Aunt Maud was dying.

Muff said, 'Dadda was there to begin with, to help me, he had compassionate leave when Grace died, but after that, though he was posted further south, near to Chester, and came whenever he could, I was really tied to the cottage, hand and foot, several months. Maud couldn't be left day or night, the poor darling. Hermione came to sit with her sometimes when one of the Dobson girls was free to look after her children, but of course I had to catch up on sleep then, and she must have been lonely. She was such a lively, warm and outgoing person, she needed to talk, be in company. Especially at that particular time! It's extraordinary how things come in threes! That old superstition! Grace dying, then Maud, then the news about Gilbert! He'd been taken prisoner. Hermione had a card from a camp in North Italy. She didn't tell me at the time, I suppose she thought I had enough on my plate, but I do wish she had. I think now she must have been . . . *desperate*!'

Muff hesitated over this word, frowning a little. 'Deeply unhappy, anyway. She didn't love Gilbert. I knew that by then – not from anything she had actually said, but from what she didn't say. Another woman always knows that kind of thing! She never spoke about him, about the things they'd done together, the life they had led. She never said, *Gilbert says*. I think, when she heard he'd been captured, she may have felt guilty because she didn't really care, in her heart.'

Pleased with this interpretation, she smiled at Bridie and lifted her chin. 'Might as well take the bull by the horns, dear! I expect you think I'm making too much of this ! Trying to excuse her for being unfaithful. But you know, we did take these things more seriously in a moral way, then, and I don't want you to think she was a loose sort of woman. Or a careless one, either.' A wave of delicate pink rose up her neck but her clear eyes looked bravely at Bridie. 'I mean by that, she did take steps not to get pregnant. She used her cap. But the jelly she put on it was stale, or perhaps there wasn't enough of it. There was nowhere she could have got fresh supplies, the chemist in the village didn't keep that sort of thing, and without the jelly, of course, you might as well put a lettuce strainer on your head for all the good it would do!'

This detail, and the sad little joke, was clearly an effort. Bridie said, 'Dearest Muff, you don't have to go on! I believe you. I believe she was a nice person. A good woman – a saint, if you like! Do you know who my father was?'

Muff locked her fingers together and looked down at them. She breathed deeply. Bridie saw her frail chest expand, fluttering the soft, white silk of her blouse. She let out this long breath in a soft, puffing sigh and said, 'He was the young Italian who worked on the Dobsons' farm, darling. I'm afraid I can't tell you much more than that. He went to the farm, from the prison camp, some months before Gracie died, and though of course I'd *seen* him a few times, I can't say I knew him. He was good looking, good mannered – like a lot of those prisoners, very polite, very courteous. That was quite a little joke among the farmers' wives locally. The Italians would do things for them, carry heavy buckets, that sort of thing, that would never occur to their husbands! This young man, Mario, once mended my bicycle and spoke to me very pleasantly. His English was good. Hermione told me he was well-educated, even though he was an ordinary soldier. But she didn't tell me that until quite a lot later. I didn't even know she was pregnant, not for a long time.

She leaned back, looking tired. The leather photograph album slipped on her lap. Bridie took it and put it on the table beside her. She said, 'Rest for a minute. I'll make some tea, shall I?'

She thought she had never loved her mother – *my mother*, she thought defiantly – as much as she did at this moment. And yet to say so seemed an intrusion. She could only make tea for her, choosing the prettiest china, opening a fresh packet of biscuits. When she came back with the tray, Muff hadn't moved; was still sitting, hands clasped, little feet side by side on the stool. But the rest had restored her. There was colour in her cheeks, a bright look in her eyes.

She said, 'Aunt Maud was ill for six months. It was hard for her to begin with, she'd been such a strong, active woman, and for a while at the end, when she fought for her breath, but in between she was peaceful, simply drifting a little further down every day. Hermione left four weeks before the end came. I thought I heard the postman one morning and came down and found a note on the mat. She hadn't wanted to disturb me in case I was busy with Aunt Maud or sleeping, but she wanted me to know she'd decided to go off for a while to visit some cousins in Shrewsbury. I'd never heard of these cousins. I'd always understood that Hermione had almost no family. No one close, anyway. She was an only child and her parents were dead. But she gave me this address, so I wrote and said I was sorry I hadn't seen her, but I'd keep in touch, let her know what was happening. I assumed to begin with that she'd be coming back to the farm but Mrs Dobson came up with some eggs and said Mrs Lash had left for good as far as she knew, packed up, paid an extra month's rent, and gone. Mrs Dobson was a bit stiff and I wondered if there had been some disagreement between her and Hermione but I was too taken up with Aunt Maud to think much about it. It wasn't until she was dead, after the funeral, when I wrote to Hermione again and still had no answer that I started to worry.

She sipped her tea, crumbled a biscuit. 'I had nothing to keep me. I got on the bus to Shrewsbury, found the address. A little house in a back street – as soon as the woman opened the door, I knew who she was! She'd been cook in Hermione's parents' house. I'd been to stay there several times, half terms from school, and the cook always sent us back with a cake, pots of jam. She was a lot older now, over sixty, but she still had the same dark red hair piled up high – not a strand of grey in it. I'd changed much more, I thought, but she recognised me, asked me in. She lived in this house with her father and Hermione's children were with her. This was early afternoon and they were both still at school. She said that Hermione had asked her to look after them; she'd decided to do something to help the war effort and had gone to Bristol to work in munitions. She'd left money for the children and promised to visit them but she had written a couple of days ago and said that she couldn't come for a while because she was ill. Nothing really serious, she said, a grumbling appendix, but the doctor had said she should have it out as soon as he could fix it up at the hospital. This woman, the cook – I can't remember her name now – didn't seem worried; she said she was fond of the children, they brought a bit of life into the house. Her old father who was sitting in the room with us, sitting by the fire, gave a bit of a chuckle. He didn't say anything then, but when his daughter went to the kitchen to make a pot of tea, he said, 'If you ask me, missus, she's got the sort of appendix that gets wheeled out on a pram.'

Muff hadn't stayed long after that. The next bit of her story was a traveller's tale that she told with some gusto. Getting about wasn't easy in wartime and she had to make an awkward, cross-country journey. Repeating the details absorbed her – how she had caught one train by the 'skin of her teeth', missed another, waited most of that night in a buffet at a railway station where a young soldier was 'so kind' to her, getting her a mug of strong tea and making her lie down to rest on a bench, folding up his greatcoat to make her a pillow. For Muff this had obviously been an adventure; watching her, only half-listening, Bridie tried to see her as she must have been then, more than thirty years ago. A few wrinkles, perhaps – she had seen her child die, her beloved Aunt Maud, those deaths must have left their marks on her – but her chin line still firm, her blue eyes set in firm, glowing flesh. Not a young woman any more, but still pretty and delicate looking, with a pretty, light laugh . . .

She had had a tiring twenty-four hours, waiting on stations, travelling in slow, jolting, cold trains, crowded with soldiers. It was dark when she got to Bristol. Winter time, and a moonless night, a blacked-out, wartime city, not a chink of light showing. Someone at the station gave her directions but she missed a turning somewhere and lost her way. She went into a public house and a man offered to take her to the street she was looking for. ('People were so kind, during the war,' Muff said, 'total strangers.') She must have looked exhausted by this time because the publican produced a bottle of brandy from under the counter and insisted that she should have a drink before going further. The drink made her giddy – she had had nothing to eat or drink for so long except tea, and the young soldier's chocolate. She drank it down and then went, with the man who had offered to show her the way, through the dark streets to the address the old cook had given her.

A woman let her in and directed her up the uncarpeted stairs of a kind of house Muff had not been inside since her days as a district nurse in the East End of London; a stained sink on the landing with a tap dripping, the only water supply for the tenants, walls bubbled with damp, a single, shared lavatory. Muff could hardly believe she would find Hermione here, in this bleak, comfortless place; she hardly recognised the thin, wild-looking creature who opened the door to her. Who stared and stared and then laughed until her voice cracked with tears and she said, 'For Christ's sake, why have you come? You, of all people!'

Muff said, 'Well, of course, I just put my arms round her. Poor, darling girl! Alone in this horrible place! It was all she could find or afford, she said, she had to pay for the children's keep, but I think, in a way, she was punishing herself. She'd been lying in this cold room, huddled on the bed in some scruffy old blankets, even though there was a gas fire. I put some money in the meter and lit the fire, made her a hot drink on the gas ring with some cocoa and dried milk I found in the cupboard, rubbed her cold hands. She wouldn't talk at first, it was almost as if she resented my coming and finding her like this, but after a little, when she was warmer, she told me about it. She had really fallen in love with this Italian, with Mario. It had started when she lent him some books; he was anxious to improve his English, and she had time on her hands once the children had been put to bed. It was towards the end of the summer, the harvest was over, but it was still light until quite late in the evening, and warm. They settled down in the orchard at the back of the farm house with the books, and of course one thing led to another. I suppose it would be easy to say it was only *sex*, she was lonely, he was a young man, far from home, but I really believe there was true love between them. He was so gentle, she said, so considerate, he would never come to her at night, in her room, for fear of disturbing the children. But it was a big farm, lots of outbuildings, plenty of places they could be quite private in. They often used to meet in the grain loft over the stables, she said – she was relaxed by this time, and she laughed like a

happy girl as she told me. It was lovely up in the loft with the
loading door open and the moon coming in and the dry smell of
grain and the old shire horses stamping and snorting below.
And they could keep an eye on the house through the open loft
door in case one of the Dobsons came out. It was important that
they never suspected, and not just for her sake, but *his*. Being a
prisoner, he was supposed to be indoors after dark but the Dobsons were easy with him and treated him like one of the family.
That was one of the reasons why Hermione left the farm when
she did. She thought Mrs Dobson had been giving her some
funny looks and she was afraid that she'd guessed. But she
knew that neither of the Dobsons would want to make trouble
for Mario unless it was forced on them. Once she'd gone, Hermione thought, it would be a case of least said, soonest mended,
as far as *they* were concerned. The other reason was that Mario
had no idea she was pregnant. Partly because he was young,
inexperienced, and partly because she'd really, at the beginning, hidden it from herself in a way. *Pretended* – until she knew
she was starting to show. Then she went, in a hurry. She didn't
tell Mario – there was no point, since she had made up her mind
what to do – and there was no time to lose. She intended to have
the baby adopted and that meant her children, Matthew and
Cassie, must know nothing about it.'

'In case they told their Papa when he came back from the
war?'

'Don't laugh, Bridie! It was a real problem. Pray God you
never have to face anything like it! She wasn't only thinking of
herself. She had Matthew and Cassie. If Gilbert found out –
well, any man, I suppose, but Gilbert *especially*, with his brutal
nature – there would be no life worth living for anyone! What
she did was very brave, really. Going off on her own, telling no
one, not even me, though she must have known I'd have helped
her. She said she hadn't wanted to involve me, but I think it was
something else, too; she wanted to punish herself, as I said, to
sink down. Finding this dreadful room, barely eating! I spent
the night with her, shared her bed as we'd done so long ago,

when we were at school, in that other war, and went out the next morning to buy food for her, but she wouldn't have much, even then, just a slice of bread, a glass of milk. I could see she wasn't fit to be left. I couldn't take her back to the cottage with me. The only thing I could think of was to go back to London. My father and mother were still there, in the vicarage. They'd stayed there, of course, all through the bombing. Though the church had been hit, and the houses around . . .'

Thinking of her parents, Muff smiled. 'You won't remember them, I know, you were too young when they died, but they were such good, resolute people. The house was full, all through the war, of refugees from Europe, neighbours who had lost their homes, but they always had room for someone who needed them. It was a happy house, even though there was so much sadness all round it, the rubble, the bomb sites, the little shops boarded up, piles of sandbags, and I think Hermione was happy there. We both were. As happy, though in a different way, as we had been in Shropshire. There was so much we could do to help and it was good for her to feel useful; she helped my parents and they helped her. They'd seen so much misfortune and they were so practical. And, somehow, *impersonal*. Even though they were sympathetic and kind, they kept a distance, a sort of perspective about human behaviour that was very consoling. They weren't concerned with delving into the past – psychoanalysis would have been a great waste of time in their view! – only in making the best of things as they were. They trusted in God, believed in an after life, and didn't expect things to be perfect in this world. Hermione's situation wasn't unusual in wartime – nor at any time, come to that! – and once she had told them what she intended to do with the baby, they accepted her decision as the only one possible and supported her in it. My father saw she was booked into hospital, gave her the address of a good adoption society, and that, as far as he was concerned, was the end of the matter. I suppose, if things had gone smoothly, if she had been delivered in hospital, it would have been, too. But it didn't happen like that, she went into labour one evening, and it was all over so quickly! The baby was born before the ambulance came!'

Muff laughed. She sounded like a young woman. She said, 'I don't know why I said, the baby! *You* were born. I delivered your mother. I was the first person to hold you. I said, to Hermione, "She's beautiful, darling, you have a dear little girl." She turned her head on the pillow and said, "Do you want her?" I couldn't think what she meant for a moment. Then she said, "Why not, O Friend of my bosom," and I looked at her, and she seemed like a little girl again, making that silly old joke, but she was a grown woman now and I saw that she meant it, that she had been thinking about this for a long time and had only now found the courage to say it. And I knew that it had been in my mind as well, but hidden, crushed down. I loved you already, so small in my arms, and I loved Hermione, too! It suddenly seemed so simple, so obvious! I said, "Of course, I'll have to ask Martin," and she laughed and said, "My dear idiot, he'll do anything for you!"

The ambulance came then and she was taken to hospital. I kept you and fed you. It was what she wanted. I was happy and frightened – terrified that something would go wrong. That she'd change her mind! Suppose Gilbert died in the prison camp – she might want to keep you! I was ashamed, thinking these things; I felt guilty, being so happy! Then Martin came and went to see her in hospital and I waited for him, sure he'd come back and say it was no good after all. When he came in the door, I was afraid to look at him, but when I did look, he was smiling. He said, "It's all right, she's our daughter." He arranged everything, all the papers. I wanted to keep in touch with Hermione, send her pictures of you, but Martin said no. When she left the hospital she was going straight to her children in Shrewsbury. She didn't want to see me again and she didn't want letters or photographs. It was the best way for us all, he said, and the kindest to her. A clean break . . .'

Muff sighed. 'All I've heard of her since is what I've seen in the newspapers. She published a book after the war – I opened the paper one morning and there was a picture of her, and a little piece, saying she had started writing to support her family when her husband came home from a prison camp too ill to work. She's written quite a lot since, women's novels I suppose you would call them, romantic stories, boy meeting girl and all ending happily. Although they seem sad to me in a way, knowing how her own love affair ended, and what her life must have been like since then. Until Gilbert died, anyway. I saw his death in *The Times*. That was about ten years ago, I can't remember exactly, but you were married by then and Pansy was born. I wrote to her through her publishers saying that you were well, and the baby, her grandaughter, but she didn't answer . . .'

She looked at Bridie. 'Don't be hurt, darling. I don't know what your plans are, but you must understand, she may not want to see you. She's old, like me. Seventy. I suppose it's only because I've been talking about a time when we were both still fairly young, but, you know, I can hardly believe it!'

Bridie said, 'I don't think I do want to see her!'

She answered instinctively, roughly, and was immediately shocked to hear her own voice sounding so angry. Why was she angry? She had wanted to know, hadn't she? She shouldn't be angry because she had been told so much more than she had ever expected. Her life had acquired a whole new dimension and she needed time to take it in, that was all!

She said, 'I'm sorry, Muff. Thank you for telling me. I'll take it in presently. Just at the moment I feel it was stupid to ask you because now I know, it seems so unimportant. All the time you've been talking, *most* of the time anyway, what I've been interested in hasn't been *her*. She doesn't matter to me. Only *you*.

Muff said, 'You must make up your own mind, my darling.'

She was smiling but it seemed to Bridie that there was a certain reserve in her smile. Bridie was afraid, suddenly. She wanted to say, 'This won't make any difference to us, to you and me, will it?' But she remembered how scornful she had felt when Aimee had said something similar . . .

Muff was eyeing her critically. She said, 'Dearest, your cheek still looks very sore. I really think you ought to bathe it again and put some kind of soothing cream on it.'

Chapter Five

The red brick Victorian cottage that had once belonged to Aunt Maud stood some way above the road, built into the side of the bare, heathery hill that rose steeply behind it. Whoever lived there now (the crazy paving path and the tidy beds of late roses suggested to Bridie a neat, retired couple) had cropped the hedge low with a mechanical cutter and rooted out all the old apple trees, but there must always have been a good view from the upper windows over the tops of the trees and across the wide, peaceful valley. At one of them Muff had stood watching for the red handkerchief she had told Hermione to wave from her window if she was lonely. Now she could simply have telephoned, Bridie thought practically; a wire with a cluster of small birds roosting silently on it ran from the eaves of the plum-coloured slate roof to a telegraph pole by the gate.

Apart from the telegraph poles and a line of electrical pylons marching gauntly across the ploughed, autumn fields, this calm, rural landscape seemed much as Muff had remembered it. Noisier, perhaps, with the constant chugging of tractors, but otherwise Muff would find little difference. Even the small shop that she had told Bridie to look for, that marked the end of the lane that led to the Dobson's farm, was still there; an old black and white house set sideways on to the road with a weathered board advertising Hovis bread on the wall and a single petrol

pump on a strip of grass outside the front door. Bridie had
passed this landmark half a mile back and been amazed that
she had recognised it at once, without any doubt. She hadn't
stopped; she had driven on, her heart quickening to find the
map of Muff's past unrolling so clearly before her. A white gate
that led on to the bare, open hill, a tall copper beech, and
beyond it, the cottage.

Bridie stood on the road and looked up at it. A pity about the
apple trees, but Muff would be happy to hear that the house
was trim and well cared for and that the old iron seat where
Aunt Maud had so often sat to be photographed with her dogs
still stood against the wall by the porch. Bridie wondered what
had happened to the dog kennels which, according to Muff, had
filled the garden at the back of the cottage, and if the new
owners had made many changes inside it. Earlier, she had
thought she might knock at the door, picturing some kind, elderly countrywoman opening it and showing her round, perhaps
offering her tea, or a glass of home-made elderberry wine. If she
were very old, she might remember Aunt Maud who must have
been a well known local 'character'. Now, even the thought of
lifting the latch on the gate made Bridie's mouth dry. What
could she say, after all? My mother once lived in this cottage?
Suppose this woman – this *imaginary* woman, she reminded herself – knew that Muff's only daughter had died here?

A more general embarrassment seized hold of her. Why had she
come on this pilgrimage? It seemed foolish, suddenly. She had
offered to drive to South Wales to pick up Aunt Florence
and take her to London to wait for Blodwen's arrival, and
this part of Shropshire, while not exactly on the way was
not too far out of it, either. But the whole expedition was,
really, unnecessary. Although Florence had an arthritic hip,
the Mudd family were scornful of 'giving in' to the aches
and pains of old age. Florence had been perfectly prepared
to travel by train as she had made indignantly clear when
Bridie had telephoned. 'I suppose you think I'm too old to stand
on my own two feet! Or is it your Father who's put you up to it?

Poor old Florence, ready for the scrap heap!' She had only accepted as a favour to Bridie. 'Well, if you've got the time to waste, I suppose I don't mind!' Bridie had put up with this grudging response, uncomfortably aware that fetching her aunt was only an excuse for this detour to Shropshire. Now she thought – What on earth *for*? What am I after?

She got back in the car – James's car, one of their 'joint possessions' that he had finally given her. He didn't need it, as he would be living abroad, but he had made a great production out of his generosity, driving the car to Islington early one morning before she was up and posting the keys through the letter box with a note saying, *Herewith one much loved family chariot, cleaned and wax-polished and hoovered inside. Perhaps you will endeavour to take care of it, if only for reasons of sentiment.* Bridie had wept tears of rage and been glad to discover that the yearly motor tax was about to run out and that the car needed new tyres and a new exhaust system. As she had written to James, *more than sentimental care seemed required.* Remembering the pleasure the formation of this phrase had given her, the eagerness with which she had drafted the ironic letter of thanks she had sent him, she wondered if she were really quite as free of James as she'd thought. Oh, of course she was free of him, she told herself sturdily; the occasional outburst of impotent rage was of no more account than an itch from an old wound that had healed with astonishing speed. Or perhaps it was as her father had said: she was bored and casting round for some way to kill time. Sending James silly letters, setting out on this journey . . .

She backed into the white gateway, turned the car, and drove back to the shop. She needed petrol and, since she left the last village, she had seen no garage, no filling station, only the single pump outside the black and white house. It was curious, she thought, how empty the country was: no one about, on the roads, in the fields, no sign of human life except the distant throb of the tractors. Even the farms she had passed seemed oddly deserted and tidy, unlike the farms of Muff's memory where pigs and chickens and geese roamed free in the yards and horses poked their mild, lovely heads over stable doors. Well of course things had changed, after all. Times had moved on and the kind of picturesque farming that Muff remembered so fondly had gone for ever. Hens were more productive, poor things, shut up in batteries (though why *poor things*, who knew what hens felt?) and machines were more efficient and cheaper than horses and men. Presumably the shop where Muff had bought her weekly wartime rations had been altered and modernised, too: there would be a deep-freeze full of crinkle-cut chips, frozen peas, cod steaks, ice cream; tinned meat, sliced bread, packaged biscuits; a formica counter instead of the cool marble slab on which old-fashioned grocers used to measure out butter, cutting and shaping and slapping with neat, wooden pats.

Not that the shop, a lean-to against the side of the house, looked as if many improvements were likely to have been made inside it. All that was displayed in the fly-spotted window was a dusty pyramid of soup tins and a large cardboard stand featuring a dimple-bottomed infant and advertising baby cream. An iron bell hung from the wall by the window to summon attention but as Bridie only wanted petrol, she stayed in the car and tooted her horn.

And, at once, felt sick with anxiety. Muff had told her that this shop had been kept by a middle-aged couple who had run it as a sideline to a small holding, selling their own eggs and milk and vegetables as well as bread and groceries. It sounded to Bridie like the kind of undemanding and healthy life that might lead to a prolonged and active old age. 'Oh, don't be a fool, for God's sake,' she said aloud, in a firm, commanding voice, trying to calm her churning stomach, her wildly thumping heart. Even if a pair of sharp-eyed, long-memoried ancients should appear, what was she frightened of? That they would recognise her as Hermione's daughter? Of course not! Muff had known she was coming here, on this sentimental journey, this quest! If she had thought Bridie resembled her mother so closely that someone might remark on it, she would surely have warned her! No, she had nothing to fear on that score; she would not be caught out! Nor need she feel *guilty*! She was not doing anything wrong . . .

All the same, when the door of the house opened, her head spun with terror. But it was only a girl, wearing a frilly, flowered apron over her tight jeans, and dark sweater. Bridie managed a smile and asked for four gallons. Watching the girl work the pump, her pulse quietened, her stomach grew quiet again. She was hungry, she realised. The girl came to the car window. Bridie paid her and said, 'Do you sell chocolate?'

The girl shook her head. 'The shop's closed. Closed up. We just run the pump to oblige. When we bought the house the old shop went with it. It hasn't been open, really, for a long time. Not since the old fellow took bad. He was going on eighty. But it's surprising how many people still stop, though it doesn't look very enticing, does it, what's in the window?'

She smiled; her friendly smile and her pretty, lilting Welsh voice encouraged Bridie.

She said, 'Do you know anywhere, a farm, that lets rooms in the summer? A cousin of mine brought her family here – oh, a few years ago now. She said there was a shop near the farm where the children bought sweets. I thought that this might be the shop, from the way she described it.' She widened her eyes artlessly. 'Is there a farm down that lane?'

'Fowlers Farm,' the girl said. 'But they wouldn't take summer visitors.' She smiled her friendly smile. 'It's a show place!'

Bridie crinkled her eyes up. She said, speaking slowly and thoughtfully, 'Dobson. I *think* that was the name. What my cousin said.'

'Not at Fowlers. They're people called Newhouse. I don't know any Dobsons round here. But I'm from Aberdare, only been here three years.' She laughed. 'The way folk round here look at it, that makes me a foreigner!'

Bridie laughed with her. 'Oh, I *know*! Country people!'

She felt very cheerful. If the Dobsons had still lived at the farm she didn't think she would have dared to drive past it.

How stupid she was to have been so alarmed, she thought. All she needed was a good alibi and she had one to hand now! She was a woman with several young children, looking for a good place to take them for next year's summer holiday, driving round this pleasant country where her cousin had stayed some years back and had such a happy time. Dorothy, she thought. Dorothy Ardway. That was the cousin's name. If you fleshed out your lies they became more convincing in your own mind and more likely to convince other people.

Dorothy had three children, Bridie decided, two girls and a boy (she would give them names in a minute!) and her husband was a nuclear physicist. Henry. Sebastian. Sir Sebastian Ardway, the Nobel prize winner? No – that was getting too fancy. A knighted physicist sounded too old for the good-looking man in his mid-thirties she was envisaging. Henry Ardway would do very well. Dorothy was still a vague character to her, but Henry began to develop. Tall, slender, blue-eyed, very clever, an excellent swimmer. Perhaps *he* was her cousin, not Dorothy, Bridie thought. She and Henry had played together as children. Their parents (the mothers were sisters!) had taken a house by the sea, in Cornwall, perhaps, and Henry had taught her to swim. He was eighteen months older than she was, and when she was growing up she had been a little in love with him.

Waving goodbye to the girl, Bridie thought – *This family game!* It was one she had played all her childhood, inventing relations, giving them names, ages, accomplishments, precise physical details, holding long conversations with them in bed. An adopted child's fantasies? More likely an only child's longing for brothers and sisters, she told herself, remembering, as she turned into the lane, that she *did* have a brother. A half-brother, anyway. Half-brother Matthew, half-sister Cassie who had, presumably, run up this very lane to the shop to buy their war-time sweet rations, fished for newts in this ditch, gathered cob nuts, rose hips and blackberries from the tall, flowery hedges, reaching up sticks to the best fruit, the high branches . . .

There would have been hedges then, she supposed, as well as the horse-chestnut trees Muff remembered that had showered down Gracie's 'fat conkers.' Now only electrified cattle fences ran along the bare tops of the steep banks either side of the lane. She drove downhill between these steep banks for about a third of a mile, splashed through a shallow brook that bubbled over the road, and began to climb up again. A house appeared on rising ground on the right of the lane and a field full of cows on the left. They were pretty cows, Bridie noted, with dainty horns and delicate legs. Even without the elegantly lettered notice on the farm gate that said, *The Newhouse Herd, Mr. John Newhouse, Mr. Charles Newhouse*, she would have known those cows were aristocratic! She stopped the car by the gate and looked at the house. Large, square, painted white – nothing grand about it but it was a good house, well-proportioned, well kept, like the outbuildings and the swept, gravelled yard.

Bridie got out of the car. Her legs felt slightly unsteady but she had no other nervous physical symptoms. Talking to the girl at the shop had given her confidence. If anyone should appear, she had her story prepared. Dear Henry and Dorothy Ardway had spent such a happy holiday somewhere round here. No one would know that she had already been told that they didn't take summer visitors at Fowlers Farm.

She pushed open the gate and crunched over the gravel. It made a surprising amount of noise under her feet. She stopped halfway across the yard and looked round with what she hoped would appear, to anyone watching her, an innocently speculative air. But there was no sign of life from the house, or from the handsome old barn, blank-walled on this side except for a small, green-painted door high up, under the eaves. Was that the loading door to the grain loft where Hermione had lain with her lover? There had been stables below, Muff had said; horses, snorting and munching and stamping. Bridie walked round the side of the barn and came on the working part of the farm, out of sight of the house; an orderly yard with a manure heap, a tractor shed, a wire chicken run where (she was glad to see) plump hens were happily scratching. The big barn was a dairy parlour now, with named stalls. Maria, Clementine, Rose of Genoa, Flower of Rome. A hum of machinery came from behind a closed door at one side of the entrance; on the other, there was a plain, wooden staircase.

She stood at the foot of the stairs, looking up. If they led to the loft, she ought to feel something! Hermione – *poor Hermione*, she made herself think, conscientiously, had crept up these stairs in the sweet, summer dusk, heart thudding with passion, with fear of discovery. She had been happy, Muff said, but she must have understood the terrible risk she was running, the appalling irony of it! Making love to her handsome Italian while her husband was in an Italian prisoner of war camp! It was unforgivable, really! She wasn't a girl, she was thirty-eight – old enough people would say, to know better. She could hardly plead youth and innocence, blame her seducer. If the Dobsons had caught her, she would have been so humiliated. Such an undignified situation for a middle aged, middle-class woman, with a husband and children, a respectable place in society. Romping in farm yards, fucking in grain lofts, abandoned to joy in hay stacks and orchards . . .

Bridie felt hot with rage suddenly, anger and envy burning inside her and turning, almost at once, into an uprush of sexual yearning that seemed to drain the blood from her body; made her limbs jerk and tremble. Faint with longing, damp with desire, she leaned against the wall of the barn, fists clenched in the pit of her stomach. It would pass. The pain – the lovely pain – would pass in a minute. What a waste, she thought, what a pity! Ridiculous, also, to think that it was jealousy of her own mother that made her so randy! So helplessly, hopelessly; such profitless anguish! She whispered, 'She was thirty-eight, ducks, older than you, there's hope for you yet,' trying to make herself laugh, but she only wanted to weep. She uncurled her fists, fumbled for a handkerchief in her blazer pocket and blew her nose loudly.

'Can I help you?' a man said behind her. He sounded polite;

mildly surprised. She turned, startled. Blood rushed to her face. How long had he been here?

'Well, yes, you could,' she said. The ambiguity of this exchange made her giggle foolishly. Any man who wasn't repulsive, or old, could help her just at this moment, and this man was quite young. About Adrian's age, a bit older, perhaps. Certainly *tidier*, Bridie thought wildly. Not very tall, not much taller than she was, but neatly made, neatly dressed in a brown sweater and beautifully fitted cord trousers. Realising that she was staring at his fly, she giggled again. Stop that silly, ridiculous noise, she told herself and, with an effort, lifted her eyes to his face. A blue eyed young man with straight, smooth, fair hair, was looking enquiringly at her, apparently unaware of (or unconcerned by) the lustful way she was gazing at him. Well of course, she thought, women were lucky that way. How they felt didn't show! But she was conscious that the old shirt she was wearing under her blazer had shrunk last time it was washed and was revealingly tight. Her nipples poked through the thin wool like round buttons. She hugged her arms across her chest and said in a rush – abandoning Henry and Dorothy and their three un-named children – 'I'm terribly sorry. I'm not really trespassing. It's just that I've been driving about and seem to have lost my way and I thought there would be someone about in the farm yard to ask. But there doesn't seem to be. I mean, of course, that until now there wasn't.'

Amazingly, he seemed to accept this. He said, 'Where are you making for?' He took a pair of spectacles out of his back trouser pocket and put them on, pushing them up the bridge of his nose with his finger. He smiled at her. 'That's better.'

'Better?' she asked vaguely. Oh God, she was thinking, where am I going? Her mind was quite blank. She said, 'Well, I'm not absolutely sure, *actually*,' and groaned inwardly. Must she speak in that ghastly, fluting, debutante's voice? The name of the last village she had passed through came to her and she seized on it. 'I was thinking of staying in Castle Stoke for the night. That's somewhere near here, isn't it? Someone told me, a friend of mine said, there's a nice little pub there. I can't remember the name.' She frowned artificially. 'It'll come in a minute.'

'The Welsh Lamb—?'

'Yes. Yes, of course. That's it. How *silly* one is! I mean, the way one forgets! Though I haven't rung them, or anything. They may not be able to take me.'

'I should think they'd have a room at this time of the year.'

'*Good*!' She beamed at him enthusiastically. He seemed to be looking at her with more interest now he had put on his glasses. Short-sighted, obviously! Thank goodness, she thought, deeply grateful. She said, 'Is it far?'

'About three miles along the main road. You'll have to go back up the lane. You could go on but it's a little more complicated.'

They walked round the barn and across the gravelled yard in front of the house to the gate. In the lane, a new, green, Saab car stood behind her old Renault.

Bridie said, 'Oh, my goodness, I'm terribly sorry! You wanted to drive in and I've blocked you.'

'Don't worry. I can't get past you, the lane is too narrow, but if I open the gate you can drive in and turn in the yard. I'll move my car on.'

He opened her car door. She edged past him, trying to avoid touching him, which was difficult since there was so little room between the car and a fairly deep ditch. She could smell the wool of his sweater, damp with the soft, autumn air He closed the door and she wound the window down, leaving her hand on the top of the glass. He put a hand beside hers. Their little fingers touched briefly. A shiver ran down her arm. He said, 'Sorry,' and moved his hand further along. They both laughed, self-consciously. He said, 'You know, I think, the way we're positioned, it would be better if you backed into the yard. Can you manage that?'

'Oh, I think so.'

'All right. Go back up the lane and turn left when you come

to the road. If you have any trouble at the Welsh Lamb, tell them I sent you.'

She looked at his hand which was small for a man's, with gingery hair sprouting on the backs of his neat, stubby fingers, and shining, pink nails. If he was a farmer, he was a farmer who went to a manicurist.

She said, 'Are you John or Charles Newhouse?'

'Neither. They're my father and brother. I'm Philip.'

'My name is Bridie. Bridie Starr.'

He smiled down at her. There was a small space between his front teeth. He said, 'What a pretty name.'

She was embarrassed to find she was blushing again. She said quickly, 'You don't work on the farm, then?'

He shook his head. 'I help weekends, sometimes. Unskilled labour. I know one end of a cow from another, that's about all.' He was staring at her, still smiling. He said, 'How do you get on with her?'

'Her?'

'The Renault. I used to have one. An old Renault Four. Splendid old girl. Did a hundred and thirty thousand miles before she departed this life. Went to that Great Garage in the sky.' She saw he was blushing, too. Perhaps it was infectious. 'Sorry,' he said. 'I don't know why I said that. I'm not really anthropomorphic about cars.'

'Do you like the Saab?'

'Very much. Lovely on the motorway. Though I still miss the little Renault in London. Parking, and so on.' He took his hand from the window. 'Well. I expect you want to get on. The light's going.'

'Yes.'

'Good luck at the Welsh Lamb.'

'Thank you.'

'They do quite a good meal. Really excellent home made soups. And there's a snug little bar.' He paused, cleared his throat. 'If you do decide to stay there, you might tell them, the couple who run it, that I'll probably drop in later on. After dinner.' He laughed uncertainly. 'I usually do on Saturday nights, when I'm here for the weekend.'

'Yes, I'll tell them.'

She switched on the ignition and put her foot hard down, racing the engine. He said something inaudible. She smiled gaily and backed the car into the gateway, making the gravel fly. He held his thumbs up, then waved, and ran to the Saab. As he drove past the gateway she shouted, 'Maybe I'll see you then,' but though he glanced at her, smiling, she thought that he hadn't heard her. As soon as he had cleared the way she put the car into first gear and swept out of the yard with a flourish, only just missing the gatepost.

She had been happy in bed with James to begin with, on their honeymoon and for several months after, energetic, excited, astonished by physical pleasure, crying out, 'Oh, how lovely, how lovely that was, I wish we could go on for ever.' One night he had said – laughing quite kindly – 'Sorry, goose, can't oblige, it's not so easy for me, it never is easy for a man, breaking in virgins,' and she saw she had made herself ridiculous with her silly enthusiasm, throwing her great limbs about like a clumsy girl on a hockey field, panting and moaning. The first time they'd made love after Pansy was born he had praised her, saying how much better it was for him now, so much more room since she'd had her baby, but though she had tried to respond she had shrivelled, dried up with shame. After that she had only enjoyed sex with him when she was drunk; had trained herself not to want it.

Or thought she had. Lying in a hot bath at the Welsh Lamb before dinner, she was surprised and delighted to find she was still excited. She caressed herself tenderly, careful not to bring herself to a climax. It was so good to feel sexy again, open and ready for love, she didn't want to lose it too soon. So much went with the physical feeling, a sense of pure glowing well-being, of calm happiness that took pleasure in everything: the little pub with its leaping fire in the bar, her pretty bedroom overlooking a churchyard, the warm bathroom papered with pink cabbage roses, the delicious smells rising up from the kitchen beneath her. The whole world looked different, she thought, full of promise; she was looking forward to her dinner, to the rest of the evening, to the rest of her life. She felt charged with joy, like an electric current. When Philip Newhouse touched her hand, had he felt it tingling between them? She groaned with happy embarrassment, sank briefly under the lovely, hot water, wallowing, blowing bubbles, then heaved herself up and got out of the bath, wrapping her towelling robe round her. Regarding her hot face, gleaming with health in the mirror, she said in a comic voice, 'Well, there's one thing, me old duckie-doodle, it does wonders for the complexion.'

She dressed for dinner, first in a green, low-necked jersey dress, one of her favourites; then took it off and put on a wool skirt and white sweater. That was the sensible thing to wear for an evening alone in a country pub, wasn't it? And an evening alone was what she intended. A quiet dinner, a quiet hour or so by the fire in the bar with a book. She had brought *War And Peace* with her, *Fear of Flying*, and, since she was driving round Shropshire, the *Collected Poems of Housman*. Which should she take down to the bar? *Fear of Flying* was too erotic, too obvious a best-seller, to be seen reading in public, and she should have read *War and Peace* years ago! She took the *Housman*, but when she was settled in the bar with her Campari and soda, she thought it looked affected to be sitting there, reading poetry, and bought four picture postcards of the Welsh Lamb to send to Muff and the children. To Adrian, to Aimee, to Pansy, she wrote the same message: she was having a few days holiday on her way to pick up Aunt Florence and was staying at 'this pretty pub.' To Muff she wrote that the weather was perfect, the countryside beautiful, and that nothing much seemed to have changed except people. She had been to Fowlers Farm and found that the Dobsons no longer lived there.

Dinner was at seven thirty. A dim light, a musty smell, and a collection of stuffed birds under a glass dome on the huge, mahogany sideboard, made the dining-room seem a bit like a tomb, but the food was delicious: watercress soup made with nutmeg and cream, and guinea fowl with game chips and a salad of lettuce and tarragon. She ate slowly, savouring the pleasure of each mouthful, and wondering if Philip Newhouse really would 'drop in after dinner.' Feeling her pulse race, she thought, *how ridiculous!* Of course it was fun to imagine she was falling in love with him (and why shouldn't she have a little fun, after all?) but anyone would do, the way she was feeling. Perhaps that was the meaning behind the old fable, the story of the Princess and the enchanted frog. If you were in the right mood, the first living creature you met, the first frog you kissed, was bound to turn into a Prince!

Not that she had kissed Philip Newhouse. Nor was she likely to. Even if he turned up, nothing could come of it, as Muff might say! When they had gone to Westbridge to collect her things, she had left her contraceptive pills in her bedside table drawer. Out of a weird kind of delicacy, she had thought at the time. Muff was in the room with her, helping her pack, watching her. She hadn't wanted her mother to think she was planning to take a lover! But really, she realised now, she had left her pills behind because she had known James would look to see if she'd taken them!

She gave a little snort of laughter and covered it up with a cough. The only other people in the dining-room were an elderly couple, a plump woman in a purple dress, a plump man, both eating in glum, married silence. The man was picking his teeth; when Bridie laughed, he glanced at her furtively and put down his toothpick. She smiled at him sweetly, wondering if he still made love to his wife, and if he was any good at it.

After dinner, she went into the bar and sat by the fire with a glass of malt whisky. She felt calm and comfortable, watching two men playing darts, listening to the fat, slow tick of an old clock on the wall. She would wait until nine o'clock, she decided. Then she would go to bed and read *Fear of Flying*. It was undignified to hang about. Although of course it didn't *look* as if that was what she was doing. There was nothing wrong, after all, in sitting by this pleasant fire, digesting her dinner and dreaming. Perfectly normal behaviour! In fact, it would be *abnormal*, wouldn't it, to go to bed quite so early? She might wait a bit longer, until half past nine, say, and have some more of this excellent whisky. It wasn't as if she had drunk wine with her meal, mixing the grape and the grain. Whisky was good for you, better than a sleeping pill, and even if it wasn't, even if it was *bad*, she had a right to sit here and get drunk if she chose. It was Dadda's puritanical attitude towards alcohol that made her feel guilty about it. One small sherry was all he had ever allowed her when she was growing up; even after she married he had seldom offered to re-fill her glass, though perhaps that was simply because it didn't occur to him. Dadda wasn't a drinking man, not like Hermione's husband. Hermione had been afraid of Gilbert, Muff said. Watching him all the time, afraid to provoke him. Well, she could understand *that*, Bridie thought: she had felt much the same about James. She could admit it now she had left him. Was it a coincidence that she had married the same sort of man as Hermione? Or an inherited tendency? Perhaps, like her real mother, she was attracted to men with violent natures. 'Watch out in future, my girl,' she murmured, and smiled to herself.

The wall clock struck nine. On the ninth stroke Philip Newhouse came into the bar. Bridie's heart banged about in her chest but when he smiled at her cheerfully it grew calm again. By the time he had bought another whisky for her, and a beer for himself, and was seated beside her, she was feeling comfortable with him, as if they were long-established old friends.

He was not yet quite at ease, though. There was a slight flush on his fair, freckled cheeks as he made a short, prepared speech. He was sorry he hadn't answered her question sensibly when she had asked him if he worked on the farm. He didn't know why he hadn't. He had felt a clod afterwards! There was only room for one son on the farm, and his brother liked the work and he didn't. He had read law at university and was a solicitor, working in London, and specialising in Probate and Wills. Perhaps that sounded dull, but *he* found it fascinating. Not so much the legal complexities, but the way people behaved, how they felt about their possessions. It was amazing how atavistic families were; how the same pattern of behaviour came out in different generations. He put all this in the form of an apology but it seemed as if he were presenting credentials. When he had finished, he waited expectantly.

Bridie said, 'I don't think it sounds dull. All those family passions!' He smiled with delight. She smiled back and saw he was waiting for her to put her cards on the table. She looked away from his smiling face, at the bright, leaping flames in the grate, and said lamely, 'It's lovely to see a log fire, isn't it?'

'Have you looked at it properly?'

She couldn't think what he meant. Then she saw there was no smoke rising up, and, all the time she'd been sitting here, the logs hadn't shifted. It was a fake; an elaborate gas fire.

Philip said, 'It's very convincing if you haven't seen one before. But like a plastic daffodil, not quite the same once you've realised . I've never understood why, but I always feel cheated.'

'So do I!' Bridie said, in an astonished voice. Their eyes met and they laughed. She said, laughing, 'At least the food's real, you were right about that,' and described the dinner she'd eaten.

He said, 'I know their watercress soup. I've made it myself, from their recipe. I'm a good cook. I'm a greedy bachelor, so I have to be!'

No escape now! Bridie took a good swig of whisky and said that she was married at the moment but was in the process of divorcing her husband. She hoped that this sounded a natural thing to say in the circumstances and that he would not respond with some dreadful, coy remark. She closed her eyes briefly and imagined him saying, 'Aha! I guessed as much! A pretty woman like you, driving round all alone, making up to strange men!' Wagging his finger and leering. 'Please God,' she prayed silently. 'Please God, don't let him.'

When she opened her eyes she was glad to see he was gazing at the gas fire. Speaking in a calm, serious voice, keeping his distance, he said he was sorry.

She was so relieved she could have wept. 'You needn't be,' she said. 'Because I'm not.'

He looked at her and nodded; then looked at the book on the table. He asked her if she liked Housman. She said she had been very fond of him when she was young, all that beautiful sadness and death, though it seemed rather an unsophisticated taste now. Philip said he didn't care if it was, he loved Housman still. Minor poets were like popular tunes; they affected the tear ducts. 'Oh, that's so true,' Bridie said. Driving round Shropshire she had recited some of the poems aloud to herself and found the tears running down her cheeks. Wenlock Edge was umbered, and bright was Abdon Burf! Philip said that it was the use of names that was so curiously moving. Towns and rivers and mountains. 'Ludlow,' he said, 'Onny and Teme and Clun.' They exchanged lines, grinning at each other with pleasure. When they seemed to have run out of quotations, Bridie said, 'I suppose I *am* unsophisticated, really. Do you know, I haven't read *War and Peace*.'

'No?'

'No.'

She thought that later tonight she would probably play back this conversation and wince at some of the things she had said, but she didn't care. It didn't matter. What they said didn't matter. It was as if they were two people from the same country, meeting abroad, delighted to find someone else who spoke the same language She said, 'Although of course I've read *Anna Karenina!*'

'Oh, *of course*,' Philip said, and picked up her empty glass.

The bar closed at ten thirty. When Bridie stood up, her head swam. 'Goodness,' she said.

Philip put his hand under her elbow. 'Five whiskies.'

'Really?' She giggled. 'How awful.'

'Well, you're quite a big girl.'

'What's that got to do with it?'

'The amount of alcohol you can cope with depends on your body weight. But perhaps you should have some fresh air.'

'I'll see you to your car.'

It was clear and cold outside; a dark sky with a bright, sailing moon. 'Nippy,' Bridie said, crossing her arms and tucking her hands in her armpits. 'I like it, though. I like autumn. It's been so hot, all this summer.'

'You're not too cold?'

'No.'

The car park was at the side of the pub, next to the church-yard. Philip opened a wooden gate and they walked on soft turf between old, leaning tombstones.

'Abigail Davies,' Bridie read, by the moon's light. 'I wonder who she was.' She yawned hugely.

'Feeling better?'

'Mmm. I wasn't feeling bad, really.'

'Good.' He hesitated. 'Look. They'll be locking up the pub in a minute. I've got to leave early tomorrow. May I see you in London?'

'Yes.' She laughed. 'Yes, of course.'

'How can I find you?'

'There's a telephone. Not mine, it's down in the hall of this house that I'm living in, but if you ring in the morning I'll be there and I'll hear it.'

He produced a pen and what looked like an old envelope out of his pocket. She told him the number and he wrote it down. She said, 'Don't lose it.'

He shook his head, smiling.

She said, 'I'd better go in. I mean, if they lock up the pub.'

'Yes, I suppose so.'

He put his hand under her elbow again and steered her back through the churchyard gate, across the car-park to the door of the pub. He said. 'I'll ring you as soon as I can. Not immediately, next week's a bit busy. But soon.'

'Oh. Well. There's no hurry. I shan't be back for a couple of days, anyway.'

They looked at each other. She said, 'I feel very odd. I don't know . . .'

He muttered something she didn't catch, then leaned forward and kissed her. His lips, and the skin round his mouth, were smooth and soft and warm. He said, 'There!' and laughed. She saw that he was as nervous as she was and it turned her to jelly. She shivered. He said, 'You *are* cold. Go in now, sleep well,' and touched her cheek with his finger.

She sang all the way to South Wales; snatches of hymn tunes, sentimental old ballads. She couldn't remember when she had last felt so cheerful; so calmly, contentedly happy. It seemed that nothing could lower her spirits; not the long drive, nor the grey rain billowing down from the mountains, nor the familiar chill of Aunt Florence's house where even the little fire, lit in celebration of Bridie's arrival, hissed and crept with the damp.

They sat on either side of this useless fire, eating a supper of ham and salad. Florence's small, bony face, shrivelled like a nut under her thick, scraped-back hair, was red and raw with the cold. Her dentures clacked as she ate.

She said, 'I suppose you know about Harry? How I've been kept in the dark all these years? Your father finally got up his courage to tell me last night. It's been a harsh blow but it hasn't surprised me. She's always been a proud, secretive girl, your Aunt Blodwen. Well, I've made up my mind. I shan't give her the satisfaction of seeing how much she has hurt me. I shan't reproach her, I shall say nothing about it. Harry's name shall never pass my lips in her presence. She'll have nothing to reproach me with, either. All the things Mother left to her in the Will, the things we couldn't send out to Australia, are waiting for her in the spare room. The best pieces of furniture, naturally. Blodwen was Mother's favourite. At the end of her life, it

was only Blodwen she thought of. Whatever the rest of us did
for her went for nothing. It was always, "Look at the flowers my
Blodwen has sent me!" Well, anyone can send flowers. Blodwen didn't come herself, did she, even though your father
offered to pay for her fare over! At a time he could ill afford it!
But she couldn't spare her precious time, not Her Ladyship!
Still, as your father says, that's all in the past now, we've got to
forgive and forget. Let bygones be bygones, now we're all old.
Not that it's easy to think of Blodwen as an old woman! I keep
trying to picture it, how she'll look when I see her, when we
meet at the airport. But all I can see is her coming in the front
door with my Harry the day they broke the news about getting
married and broke my heart along with it. Curly dark hair
blown about by the wind and her pretty face pink as a rose. A
bit like you, now I think of it. You're very much like your Aunt
Blodwen.'

Bridie smiled. 'I can hardly take after her, can I?'

Aunt Florence put her plate aside and dabbed at her mouth
with her napkin. 'No. No – of course, I'd forgotten. You get old,
you forget.' She picked up the poker and prodded the fire. 'I
don't know why it's not burning properly.'

'It's too wet, I think.'

Florence lifted the top layer of crumbling coal with the poker,
opening up a small, glowing cave underneath. She said, 'You
used to come here when you were little, when Mother was still
alive, and she used to tell you all the old family tales. Sometimes
I used to wonder what you made of it all. Whether you ever
thought, this isn't my family! I used to think, poor little cocker!'

Bridie could remember those visits. The atmosphere of the
room, cold and stuffy at the same time, and the way Florence
had just opened up the hissing fire, brought back a scene from
one of them; a sudden flash of clear recall. She saw herself, sitting on a stool beside Granny Mudd's chair; Dadda, lying with
his legs stretched out in the chair opposite, his eyes closed, his
mouth open, snoring; Muff and Aunt Florence laying tea on the
round table, putting a white cloth over the red chenille cover

that had woolly bobbles dangling from the edges. An even younger Bridie had taken those bobbles into her mouth to suck, liking the taste of the furry wool mixed with her milky spit . . .

She couldn't remember what Granny Mudd had looked like, but she could remember that Aunt Florence had been tall and red-faced and angry-voiced and that she had been a little afraid of her. She was touched to think that this angry, red-faced aunt had thought of her as a 'poor little cocker', and worried about her.

She said, 'I don't think it ever worried me. Not then, anyway.'

She half hoped that her aunt would ask if it worried her now, but all Florence said was, 'Well, you had a happy nature, that's probably why.' She glanced at Bridie and sniffed. 'Just as well, too, the way things have gone for you lately. A hard time, by all accounts, and I must say, I expected you to show it a bit more than you do. But no one could say that your looks pity you!'

The grudging indignation of her tone expressed her concern. It was the way all the Mudds spoke to and about each other, Bridie thought; hiding their affection beneath indignation and sourness rather as peasants in primitive societies covered their children's faces from the jealous gods.

She said, 'I'm not unhappy, Aunt Florence.'

Any more positive statement seemed out of place here, though inwardly her heart soared and sang. It was nine o'clock in the evening. This time tomorrow she would be back in London. The next day, or perhaps the day after, Philip might ring her . . .

'Well, I'm glad for your sake you've been able to take it so lightly. I only hope it doesn't catch up on you later,' Aunt Florence said.

Chapter Six

For the fourth time that morning Bridie thought she heard the telephone. She leapt out of the bath, grabbed a towel and ran, dripping and shivering, to the top of the stairs. But although there was a phone ringing, it wasn't the one in the hall. Next door *again*, she thought irritably and dolefully as she trailed back to the bathroom. It was really disgraceful how thin the party walls of these houses were! People who talked nostalgically about the 'old days' when men 'took pride' in their work had obviously never lived in one of these nineteenth-century terraces. They were so shoddily built that if a front door was banged the whole row shook, and when a telephone rang all the street ran to answer it!

She had been back in Miss Lacey's flat for five days and Philip still hadn't called. Unless he had rung yesterday morning when she was out buying tinned meat for Balthazar. She had only been gone fifteen minutes, running to the corner shop and fretting in a queue while the one-eyed Cypriot served three apparently stone-deaf old-age pensioners. But Mrs Wilkes, the woman with the blonde beehive hair had been in – Bridie had seen her peek through her curtains as she left the house – and if Philip had rung she would have answered and taken a message. Bridie and Mrs Wilkes were on friendly terms now, ever since Bridie had asked her to feed Balthazar when she went to Wales.

'Any time, dearie. I work down the launderette in the after-
noons but I'm always in mornings, I'll always keep an eye on
the cat for you, just tap on my door and leave me your key. I'd
have done it for Miss Lacey if she'd ever asked but she never
did, she kept herself to herself and you don't like to offer, do
you? You never know, with that sort, how they'll take it. I've
often thought, poor old thing, perhaps she'd like a chat and a
coffee, after all she's got nothing against me, I pay my rent
regular, and it didn't seem natural, living in the same house
never speaking, but she froze me off the way she looked through
me when we met in the hall. I used to think, well, perhaps she
thinks I'm not good enough for her, she had that kind of snooty
expression, but when all's said and done, we're all human,
aren't we, and I couldn't help worrying sometimes, thinking of
her up there all alone, no family, never a soul coming to see her,
not as far as I knew. Especially in the cold weather when I could
smell that old oil stove. All she had to keep warm by, you know,
and they're not safe, are they, unless you look after them properly.'

A little of Mrs Wilkes went a long way. But even if she was
wrong about the reason for poor, frightened Miss Lacey's
'snooty expression', she was right about the oil stove as Bridie
discovered when she attempted to light it. Black smoke arose
and a terrible smell. She had bought an electric fire for the
studio bedroom when she moved in, and the kitchen could be
warmed up to a good fug with the gas oven, but the bathroom
was icy. She would have to do something about it, Bridie
thought, as she towelled herself dry and pulled on jeans and her
only really thick sweater. As soon as Philip had rung, and she
was free to go out, she would buy some kind of wall heater.
Warm clothes, too. Except for an occasional night with Aunt
Florence, she had never lived in a house without central heating
before and now winter was setting in – dark skies behind the
dome of St Paul's and the tower blocks, and dank, dripping
trees along the canal banks – she found she needed to dress
when she got up in the mornings as if she were going to spend a

day out of doors.

Of course, Philip might never ring. Perhaps he had never intended to. Perhaps he had asked for her number for the same reason that he had kissed her: as a friendly social gesture to mark the end of a pleasant evening.

If it *had* been a pleasant evening for him. He had appeared to enjoy himself and he hadn't seemed the sort of man to pretend. Though how did she know *what* sort of man he was? All she really knew was what he had told her: he was a bachelor lawyer who liked cooking, cars, and the poems of Housman. She had had a lovely time with him but she had been in the mood for having a lovely time. Lonely, sexually aroused – a woman looking for a Frog Prince! Anyone would have done, as perhaps Philip had realised after he'd left her. Perhaps he really had wanted to see her again when they said goodbye, but later on, thinking it over, playing back what she'd said, how she'd behaved, he had been alarmed by her obvious eagerness, by the way she had thrown herself at him. *Had* she thrown herself at him? She couldn't remember.

Not that it mattered. Reaching for her toothbrush, she scowled at herself in the mirror. She said, 'Grow up, girl, for God's sake, you get on my wick, you do really!' Why shouldn't she throw herself at him? He didn't have to catch her, take up her offer, unless he wanted to, did he? It was ridiculously silly and prim to hang around like some moony Victorian virgin waiting for him to make the first move. After all, he might not be able to. He might have lost her number. Or been killed in a car crash. The only way to find out and put an end to this boring suspense was to telephone *him*! He was probably listed. There were no directories in the house, as it happened, but she could go to the Post Office. Only, of course, while she was out doing that, he might ring . . .

She laughed as she brushed her teeth and spluttered toothpaste over the mirror. 'You are a prize idiot, honestly,' she told herself, quite affectionately. He had said that he might not ring 'immediately', and she had only been waiting five days. It was

Friday today. She would assume he was going home to the farm for the weekend. That would give her Saturday free to go shopping for clothes, and she would wait until the middle of next week before trying to reach him. Next Wednesday or next Thursday. In the meantime she would keep busy. Wash her hair, clean the flat, cook herself a good meal, look through the employment ads in the papers for a job that would suit an unskilled, unqualified woman in her early thirties, write to the children . . .

She had started letters to both Aimee and Pansy since she came back but had stopped after half a page. What she had written seemed curiously stilted. Her heart wasn't in it. It wasn't that she didn't love them, she told herself now; it was just that her old life, in which they had been so important, seemed so far away and long ago. And, of course, she had been listening for the telephone. Well, she would make up for it this coming Sunday when, if her assumption was correct, Philip would still be in Shropshire and unlikely to ring. She would settle down straight after breakfast and write two long letters, full of proper maternal affection and with a few amusing descriptions of life in Islington which seemed a pleasanter and more interesting neighbourhood than she had earlier thought it. She had become quite attached to some of the people she regularly saw from her window, walking their dogs along the canal, or occupying the benches. There was a couple of quite well-dressed, elderly gentlemen who always settled down with their bottles of wine and their newspapers on a seat immediately opposite between eleven and twelve in the morning, and a pair of middle-aged lovers who always took their place at midday, exchanging kisses and sandwiches and parting (when their lunch hour was presumably over) with lingering, sad, backward glances. She could make up an affecting little tale about them, Bridie thought. And Mrs Wilkes would be good for a paragraph. 'The Ancient Mariner could have learned a few tips from our Mrs Wilkes,' she might say. She would tell Aimee, too, how much she was longing to see her and the baby. He was nearly a month old and she should, really, have been to see him before! She would have to think up some convincing excuse. She had had a chest cold. A virus infection – not bad enough to keep her in bed, or even indoors, since Aimee knew, from her postcard, that she had been to Wales, but a danger for a young baby! It was rather shameful that she felt she must lie in this way, and she *was* ashamed of it! It had been stupid to let Dickie upset her; a fit of silly pique on her part. Never mind; all that was over now. She would just tell this acceptable lie and say she hoped to come one day next week if that was convenient.

She hoped that it would be convenient soon because she had another reason for visiting Aimee. Thinking about this other reason as she went into the kitchen, she gave a short, awkward laugh, picked up Balthazar who was slinkily winding himself round her ankles, and buried her embarrassed face in his fur. On Monday afternoon, after she had dropped Aunt Florence at Eaton Square, she had hurried straight on to Islington, anxious to get to the shops and the public library before they closed, stocking up with books and groceries as if she were preparing for a siege, or an illness. While she was in the library she had gone to the reference section and looked up Hermione in the Author's and Writer's Who's Who. She had felt oddly furtive doing this, and even odder – very strange indeed – when she saw, at the end of a long list of books she had never read, an address in Brighton. She had scribbled it down at the back of her diary, feeling ashamed, feeling guilty. Although there had been no one to see her except a couple of old men peacefully dozing over the newspapers, her whole body had been one burning blush.

She murmured to Balthazar, 'Life is full of coincidences, isn't it, Moggie?' He wriggled fretfully in her arms – he often appeared on her bed in the mornings and snuggled up, purring, but he seemed to dislike it when she made the advances. 'Just like a man,' Bridie said as she let him go, adding, unkindly, 'Only you're not much of one, are you?'

It wasn't much of a coincidence, really, she thought. A lot of people, after all, lived in Brighton. And she wouldn't call on her, naturally. But if she were going to Brighton anyway, to see her stepdaughter, she might just drive by and see what sort of place the old woman was living in. Though why *shouldn't* she call? Why be rigid about it? If she felt like ringing the bell while she was there, well, she would! She needn't say who she was. She could always make up some story. She could pretend she worked on a magazine and wanted to interview Hermione Lash for an article on romantic novelists. Though that hardly seemed fair. What magazine, anyway? Hermione would be bound to ask. No, it wouldn't work; *far* too complicated. Bridie said, in an agitated voice, 'Stop thinking about it, you idiot!'

A telephone started to ring. She stood for a minute, listening suspiciously, then raced down the stairs. It was her telephone this time, but it stopped as she reached it. She glared at it angrily, and, as if shamed into response, it started to ring again. She grabbed the receiver. 'Hallo?' she cried eagerly. She was shaking all over.

Muff said, 'Bridie? I'm sorry, dear. I rang just now but I thought I must have a wrong number. Did I fetch you down from the top of the house? You sound breathless.'

'I thought it was ringing next door. You can't always tell.' Bridie hoped that her disappointment didn't sound in her voice. She said, 'Darling, how *are* you. How's Florence? I'm sorry I haven't been over to see you, but I've been awfully busy.' Busy with *what*? 'A whole stack of letters waiting when I got back. I'll try and come Sunday.'

Muff said apologetically, 'We won't be here, darling. Not till quite late in the evening. Dadda thought it would be a good idea to take Florence away for the weekend to give us all a bit of a break. We're going down to the Cotswolds. Would you like to come too? I can easily ring the hotel and see if they have another room.'

'No thank you, Muff. As I said, I've got all these letters to answer. And I feel a bit bad about asking the woman downstairs to look after the cat again. Quite so soon.'

'Yes, of course. I'm glad you were able to drive down and fetch Florence. She doesn't care to admit it, but her poor hip really is painful. That's why I'm ringing now, really. She's in the bath, so she can't hear me. The thing is, we've just had a telegram from Aunt Blodwen to say she's arriving on Tuesday instead of on Friday and that's awkward for Dadda. He'd arranged to keep Friday free and he'd moved all his Friday appointments to Tuesday. You know he doesn't like me to drive, because of my silly heart, and I wondered, if you weren't too dreadfully busy, if you could possibly manage to take Florence to the airport. We'd be happy to pay for a hired car but you know Florence wouldn't accept it. You know what she is.'

'When I can't get on a bus, then it's time for a geriatric ward where I'll be no more trouble to anyone,' Bridie said in a fair imitation of her aunt's voice. 'Of course I will, darling.'

'Bless you, my love. That's a real weight off my mind.'

'You sound tired, Muff.'

'Well, perhaps I am, just a little' She gave a sharp, slightly hysterical laugh. 'Did Florence tell you about the new double bed she bought last month for Blodwen and Harry?'

'No. *Really?* Poor Florence!'

'Well, yes. I'm afraid she is brooding about it. Of course I know *why* – she's terribly upset because she didn't know Harry was dead, and the bed is something to fix on, to avoid saying so, but we've hardly talked about anything else since the day she arrived. She says it will make her look so ridiculous in front of Blodwen. It's so clearly a *new* bed, she says; a new, silk-covered quilt, new blankets, and not a mark on the mattress! She is going to tell Blodwen that she bought the bed for Dadda and me when we went down to stay with her last Easter, and she's made Dadda promise to back her up if Blodwen says anything. I don't think I'd mind that, if *he* didn't seem to take it so seriously. As if he really believed that Blodwen might march into Florence's spare room and *jeer*, the moment she sees this new bed there!'

'I suppose she might, mightn't she? I mean, neither Dadda nor Florence have been exactly complimentary about their dear sister's character! But Florence is *afraid* she will jeer, that's what matters. Dadda is just trying to comfort her and avoid any trouble.'

Muff said plaintively, 'I can't see why they don't simply say what they feel. All those Mudds. I shouldn't say this, my darling, it's disloyal to Dadda, but this last couple of days with Aunt Florence, I've felt, once or twice, that I was coming to the end of my tether! It would be so much easier if she would just admit she is hurt because she'd not been told Harry was dead until now! It must have been a dreadful shock for her. After all, in her mind, he may still have been the young man she once loved, who was stolen from her. If only she could just have a good cry and get it all out of her system! Instead of all this worked-up, angry talk about how 'small' the fact that she bought this new double bed makes her look! And the *lies* we shall all have to tell! After all, we didn't go to stay with her last Easter. Dadda and I went to Madeira for two weeks, to Reid's Hotel. Blanche and Sam know that. We sent postcards to them. And Dadda took a lot of photographs of the flowers in that lovely garden. Do you remember?'

'I remember,' Bridie said. 'But I suppose you can fix Blanche and Sam, tell them not to mention it, and you don't have to show Blodwen the photographs, do you? Or if Dadda wants her to see them, and I can see that he might, they were rather exceptionally good and he was proud of them, you needn't say *when* they were taken!' She giggled. 'Oh, I can see that it's difficult. A bit like walking through a minefield. You'll just have to try and watch where you are putting your feet!'

She had hoped to make Muff laugh, but she only sighed deeply. She said, 'Sometimes I think it's a kind of family sickness, the way everything has to be wrapped up and hidden. An inherited illness none of them can escape from. It seems a wicked thing to say, but there have been moments this week when I've wondered how Gracie would have turned out if she'd lived!'

Muff did laugh then, deprecatingly. This sour little joke was so unlike her, Bridie thought, that she must indeed be 'at the end of her tether.' Worn out by Florence already, dreading the prospect of Blodwen's arrival, of being trapped in that tiny flat with them, tangled up in their emotional labyrinths, their tireless obsessions with old loves and new beds. Poor Muff, oh *poor* Muff, with her sweet, open, straightforward nature! Bridie's heart ached for her. 'Oh, I know they're a terrible lot,' she said cheerfully, tenderly, 'but you mustn't let them get you down, darling. And for Heaven's sake don't brood about what might have happened to Gracie! After all, she was lucky enough to have *you*, wasn't she? Girls usually grow up like their mothers!'

Driving to Brighton on Sunday (wearing the new Ulla Ward suit and the Ferrogamo shoes she had bought on the Saturday) Bridie reflected that this had not been the most tactful remark in the circumstances. Muff had not seemed to take offence, she had said, 'Thank you dear, you're quite right, I'm sorry, I'm just an old silly,' but perhaps, afterwards, it might have seemed to her that Bridie had been gently putting the boot in. Reproaching her in a roundabout way for not being her natural mother. Well, not reproaching, exactly. Just suggesting that Bridie was hurt because no one could say of her that she 'took after' Muff.

She remembered what James had said about Pansy. He had had 'grave anxieties' about how she might 'turn out.' Only, unlike Muff, he had feared – or affected to fear – an unknown heredity. Bridie wondered which was worse. To know, or not to know? Presumably, if one of your ancestors was a murderer or a lunatic it might be pleasanter to remain ignorant. As James had seemed to be about *his* background, after all! He was an only child. Both his parents had been only children. His father had died young, of cancer. Apart from his mother, that vain, ageing beauty who had called her Bridie (James's little bride!) and a morose great-uncle with an enormous nose who had turned up at the wedding and told Martin Mudd how fortunate he was that his daughter was 'marrying money', Bridie had never met, nor heard James speak about, any other member of his family. For all she knew, she thought spitefully and gleefully as she careered along the Brighton Road in the old Renault, the prisons and mental hospitals of the United Kingdom were crowded with James's relations! What a pity she hadn't thought of pointing this out when he had been so disagreeable about Pansy's origins! '*Esprit d'escalier* is what you suffer from, dearie,' she told herself, and laughed.

How *silly* all this was, she thought, when she had finished laughing. It might be interesting to know who one's parents and grandparents were, trace one's biological links with the past, but it wasn't *important*! (It had been important to Oedipus, but he was a special case!) Only geneticists and genealogists were really concerned with human archaeology. Normal people (and she hoped she was normal!) did not waste their time thinking, let alone worrying, about their remote antecedents.

Just as well, too, she decided half an hour later, bending over Aimee's little boy's blue-ribboned cradle and hoping that Aimee had been too young to remember James's great-uncle. Her son's nose was rather comic and sweet at the moment, a jolly little beak on a baby, but it was clearly (at least it was clear to Bridie, who had been kissed by the old man at her wedding) a miniature replica of the great-uncle's nose. Poor little rat, she thought, seeing in her mind's eye that huge, veined protuberance growing and swelling on the tiny, red, wrinkled face like a mottled and over-ripe vegetable, what a bequest, what an inheritance!

Dickie said, 'What do you think of him, Granny? What a ghastly conk, eh? One of the Chosen Race you'd think, wouldn't you?'

'I believe Aimee's great-grandfather was Jewish, her mother's grandfather,' Bridie lied, to rebuke him. But she smiled at him kindly. In spite of that stupid remark (which was *only* stupidity, the sort of thing someone like Dickie would say

automatically, meaning no harm by it) she must try to feel
kindly towards him. He had been so welcoming when she had
abandoned her long, cheerful letter early this morning and had
telephoned instead, asking if she might drive down and see
them. 'What a super idea!' he had cried. 'If you don't mind pot
luck, come to lunch! My little wife's cooking isn't up to much
yet but I can promise you some quite decent vino!' Calling her
'Granny' was meant as a welcome, too: his way of telling her
that she had a real place in the family. Though of course it
might have crossed his mind that even if she wasn't rich like
James, or his mother, she could (unlike either of them) be called
upon to be useful in other ways. A reliable, free, baby-sitter!

Bridie put this thought from her. She didn't have to force herself to like Dickie, but there was no point in working up her dislike of him, either. He might be crude, vulgar and venal but the
main thing (the *only* thing, she told herself virtuously) was that
he was making Aimee so happy. There was no doubt about
that! Happiness spilled out of the girl's glowing face, her clear
eyes, her wide, laughing mouth. She was beamingly proud of
her baby, of her new little house with its bright cream paint and
beige wall-to-wall carpeting, of her stupid, handsome, young
husband. She hadn't realised before how handsome Dickie
was, Bridie thought. Sexy, too! His muscular body was firm as
a good apple! Even his square, money-box was attractive in an
agreeably masculine way, the lips full, smooth and glossy. A
good lover, probably. Oh, almost *certainly*! Not over-inventive,
perhaps, but eager and tireless and energetic . . .

Thrusting aside a picture of a naked Dickie leaping, penis
erect, on to her own divan bed in Miss Lacey's flat, Bridie said
hastily, 'I think the baby is beautiful. Really! Most babies have
such unformed and rubbery faces. I think his dear little nose
gives him character.'

'Darling Bridie!' As they went down the stairs from the nur-
sery, Aimee put an arm round her, hugging her tight. She
smelled milky and sweet. A sweet, milky, strong, healthy girl.
She said, 'I'm so enormously glad you approve of him! I've

been absolutely longing to show him off to you, and I was so sorry to hear you'd had such a horrid cold. Though I'm sure he wouldn't have caught it, breast-fed babies don't, do they? But you look marvellous now, you've lost a bit of weight, haven't you? And that's a lovely suit. You look lovely in it, doesn't she, Dickie?'

'I bought it yesterday,' Bridie said, eyes modestly downcast. She was afraid that if she met Dickie's gaze she would find he was leering at her suggestively.

'Smashing,' he said, indulgently, amiably. Bridie looked at him then and saw he was looking at Aimee. He said, 'What about lunch, lazy bones?' He patted his taut, young man's stomach. 'Better see to this Inner Man while His Lordship is sleeping.'

In the kitchen, a table was laid in the dining corner: lace mats on the formica, silver cutlery and wine coaster, candles, damask table napkins folded in a flower pattern.

'How pretty,' Bridie said, touched. 'Aimee, love, what a lot of trouble you've gone to!'

Aimee flushed. 'I wanted to! The first time you've been here since Baby was born. Though it's only macaroni cheese, Bridie darling. I hope you don't mind. It seems to be the one thing Dickie likes that I'm good at.'

'Oh, I don't know.' Dickie patted her bottom. 'You managed not to burn the sausages yesterday. That was quite a step forward.'

Bridie was astonished by his patronising tone. Aimee was, in fact, an excellent cook. Although the domestic arts had not been taught at the school she had gone to (girls should not be pushed into conventional, female role playing was the headmistress's fashionable view) Aimee had taken a Cordon Bleu course at the evening institute.

Aimee said, 'I'm afraid Dickie only likes plain food.' She pulled a face and laughed shyly.

'She's learning,' Dickie announced, so complacently that Bridie longed to reach over the table and slap him. Why didn't the idiot girl stand up for herself? She thought, with sudden horror, that Aimee's meekness must be her fault! She had believed she had done well by her, protecting her from James's unrealistic academic ambitions and encouraging her to do the things she enjoyed and did well, cooking and dressmaking, preparing her for what seemed her best hope of happy fulfilment, to be a wife and a mother. Now it appeared that all she had done was deliver her into the hands of a man who was determined to put her down, *denigrate* her! And Aimee had no idea how to deal with this situation because, without meaning to, Bridie had failed her. Knuckling under to James all these years, she had taught her stepdaughter subservient habits, had passed them on to her as surely as James's miserable great-uncle had passed on his hideous nose to her son! If Aimee continued to follow her bad example, let Dickie deride her without protesting, sneer at her cooking, she would turn him into a bully!

Oh, it hadn't got to that *yet*. They were still in love, still sexually happy together. That was clear from their glances, their covert smiles when their hands touched, when they brushed past each other. Perhaps Dickie really did dislike fancy food; perhaps, in spite of his healthy appearance, he had a delicate stomach. Or perhaps Aimee was educating him stealthily. The macaroni cheese was delicious, with a faint hint of garlic and spices, and the salad that went with it was a treat for a gourmet: raw mushrooms and celery and tiny, crisp, lettuce hearts, dressed with fresh basil and tarragon. As a little girl Aimee had always got her own way with James in the end Bridie remembered, as she praised the food and complimented Dickie on the beautiful bottle of wine that went with it, a rare, rich, heavy burgundy.

The wine cheered her up. Nothing, she decided, after three glasses, was as bad as she'd feared. Not everything was predetermined. Patterns of behaviour could be re-arranged, broken. We are what we make ourselves, not what others have made us! Watching Aimee feed her son after lunch while Dickie made coffee, she thought, after all, when the baby is older, he can always have plastic surgery done on his nose! She said (her line of thought running from noses, to James's great-uncle, to James) 'Aimee, darling, has Daddy been down to see you since you came out of hospital? How does he like being a grandfather?'

Neither Aimee nor Dickie spoke for a minute. Aimee took her child from her breast, put him up on her shoulder, and looked at Dickie over his little, bald head. Dickie looked at her and pulled the corners of his square mouth down. They both looked at Bridie.

She felt apprehensive. She said, 'How *is* James?' Aimee blushed brightly. Bridie said, 'He's not ill?'

They both shook their heads. Bridie looked from one to the other. 'What is it, then? Has something gone wrong about the new job?' She thought – *made* herself think – *Oh, poor James!*

Dickie said, 'Go on, Aimee.'

'I can't,' Aimee muttered. She patted the baby's back. He burped and she wiped a dribble of milk from his mouth.

Dickie sighed. 'Oh, well, then. You ought to know, Bridie. He's shacked up with his secretary. They're setting up house in Paris together next month. He brought her down here. I must say, I thought it was *cool*.'

Aimee started to cry. 'After all he'd *pretended*,' she said, between sobs. 'I mean, not making it out to be your fault exactly, but being so *sad* – I mean, that was sort of *half* blaming you, wasn't it? Going on about how you had simply walked out, how he'd had to do everything! Really such tripe! Utterly awful! Even now, what he says is, he and his new woman would never have put their relationship on this kind of footing – that's how he put it, isn't it, Dickie? – if you hadn't left Westbridge. As if you had pushed him into it! *I find I need some sort of permanent domestic arrangement since your stepmother has left me like this, high and dry*! Those were his actual words, Bridie. And in front of *her*, too. Emily. Emily Harris. That's her name. Well, you know it, of course, she's his secretary. Has been for years. I must say, I feel a bit sorry for her, in some ways. I mean, he's so utterly ghastly!' She sniffed. Dickie gave her his handkerchief. She put the baby on her lap, on his stomach, and blew her nose. 'Though I was glad that he said this in front of Dickie. I mean, Dickie hadn't understood before. He thought it couldn't have been *all* Daddy's fault. There's always *two sides*, was what Dickie kept saying. But he's seen for himself now!'

'I was deeply shocked,' Dickie said heavily. He came over to Bridie and put his hand on her shoulder, pressing it in a manly gesture of comfort. 'If there is anything I can do, I'll be glad to help. If you'd like me to talk to your solicitors. I mean, sometimes a man. . . .' He frowned. 'I mean, Adrian isn't. . . .'

'No,' Bridie said. She touched Dickie's hand and smiled up at him. She had mis-judged him, she thought. His previous attitude towards her had been perfectly natural. Newly married himself, he had been horrified to see a marriage break up. Perhaps he took a stern view of a wife's duty! He wasn't a very subtle young man. But he was moral, not venal.

Aimee laughed, rather wildly. 'One of the reasons Daddy came was to tell us that he couldn't increase my allowance. Not that we had expected it, really. Well, perhaps *I* had. A bit. But he said he might even have to cut it down! Now that he had two women to support, he said.' She gulped. 'If Emily should have to stop working.'

'Is she pregnant already?' Bridie asked. She thought – I should feel humiliated! But she only felt a kind of dry amusement. James was such a frightful old hypocrite, she thought, almost fondly, remembering the heavy performance he had put on their last night together. All that dramatic rubbish about needing his 'freedom' when all he had really wanted was a comfortable double life: secretary in Paris, little wife warming his slippers at home. Perhaps he had been ashamed because this seemed too conventional. She said, 'What's she like? I've never met her, only spoken on the telephone. James never liked me to go to the office. He said he preferred to keep his home and working life separate.'

Aimee giggled. 'She's older than you. Quite old, really, about thirty seven or eight. Not pretty, but a good figure – if she's pregnant, it doesn't show yet. Very business like. Sort of *alert* – like an eager fox terrier. She watched Daddy all the time, looking as if she might whip out a pad and a pencil and take notes any minute.'

'That's quite enough, Aimee,' Dickie said firmly. 'I really don't think Bridie wants to hear too much about her, do you?'

Aimee looked at Bridie and raised her eyebrows. Bridie shook her head discreetly. Clearly, in Dickie's view, this kind of gossip was vulgar.

She said, changing the subject to one that might suit him better, 'I don't think James should have any reason at all to cut down the allowance. He gives me a hundred and twenty pounds a month at the moment but as soon as I have a job, and I do hope to get one as soon as I can after Christmas, when Pansy's gone back to school, I shan't need it. In fact, if you're in a mess of any sort, I can probably help a bit now. I don't have any rent to pay, and apart from the car, no expenses . . .'

She reflected that the suit and the shoes she was wearing had cost almost a hundred pounds. If she added the silk shirt she had bought to go with the suit, she had spent a whole month's allowance! What on earth had possessed her? Well, of course, she had been thinking of Philip who might, one day, telephone. How shameful, how silly . . .

'I wouldn't hear of it,' Dickie said. 'We have quite enough, Bridie. As a matter of fact, as Aimee knows perfectly well, I was never all that keen on her taking that money. I mean, a man likes to feel he is keeping his wife! But I thought – *her* father, *her* business, and I can't provide all the frills she's been used to. Do you know, when we were first married, she bought something like pheasant or fillet steak just about every day! I could hardly believe it. It was like suddenly finding yourself eating at the Savoy every evening! But your position is different, Bridie, if you don't mind my saying so. My sainted father-in-law is a rich man and in spite of Women's Lib, and all that, I really do think you should check the legal position before you tell him you don't need his money. Once you've given it up, it may not be so easy to get it back, and the job market is pretty sticky just now. Although of course I agree that you should try to find something. It's very important, for your own mental health, that you should start to look forward, to make a good, new life for yourself. You're still fairly young. Young enough, anyway.'

He poured coffee into pottery mugs, passed cream and sugar, then sat down at the table and looked at her anxiously. 'I hope you don't mind my saying all this? I mean, you may think it the most abominable cheek on my part.'

'Of course I don't,' Bridie said. 'Really! Honestly, Dickie, I'm grateful.'

She did feel grateful. Ashamed, too. Dickie was so kind, so sensible. How could she ever have thought otherwise? She must look forward, look to the future. That was what she should have been doing all these last weeks instead of peering morbidly back into the past, picking over old bones. To what end, after all? Dadda had been right when he had said it wouldn't solve anything. Well, she wouldn't indulge herself any longer. She would take this nice, old-fashioned young man's advice. When she left here, she would find the street where Hermione lived and drive down it, slowing the car, perhaps, outside the place where she lived, but not stopping, and then go straight home and forget all about her.

Chapter Seven

'Your father warned me you might come,' Hermione said.
Her bulky form loomed darkly against the hanging light
in the hall behind her. She was a large woman, made to appear
larger still by the long, full, shapeless garment she wore. It was
made of a heavy, plum-coloured material that was stiff, like
canvas. Beneath it, her feet were bare. Looking down at her
bare feet (too unnerved by her opening remark to look at her
face) Bridie saw that they were elegantly slender and white;
surprisingly unmarked for such an old woman. No swollen
joints, no thick veins, no hammer toes.

Bridie said, 'I wasn't going to . . . Only – only I was passing
and I saw the police car stop, and I thought . . .'

What had she thought? Sitting in the Renault, on the opposite side of this road that climbed up from the sea, and watching
the house, like a spy? She had been alarmed when the police
arrived, but the alarm had been mixed with morbid excitement.
An agreeable sense of emergency. Oh, of course she had been
looking for an excuse! She said, 'When the policeman knocked
and you let him in, I was afraid something was wrong.' She
forced herself to look up, at Hermione's shadowed face. She
laughed, a ridiculously bright, social laugh. 'There *isn't*, I
hope?'

'No,' Hermione said. 'That is, no more than usual. Nothing

out of the ordinary. But you had better come in, now you're here.'

She stood aside, revealing the young policeman standing at the foot of the stairs. There was barely room for the three of them in the narrow hall. Both women had to press against the wall to let him pass. He stood on the front step and smiled at Hermione. 'At least you can be sure of a decent night, Mrs Lash. We'll give you a ring in the morning to let you know what time he's likely to come up before the magistrates. It depends on the list, and on how much cash he has in his pocket. I don't suppose you'll want to pay his fine?'

'No,' Hermione said.

'Then I think you can rely on his being safely locked up until the court rises.'

'That would suit me very nicely,' Hermione said. 'I could get some work done before he comes home. Thank you for letting me know.'

She closed the front door and opened another, into a small room lined with bookshelves. There was a bright fire in the grate, a heavy, handsome, gilt mirror above it, and a boy sprawled on the hearth rug, books spread about him.

Hermione said, 'I have a visitor, Benedict. You can light the gas fire in your room.'

He gathered his books and stood up. He seemed to be about twelve years old; a slight child with a round, solemn, healthy face. He left the room without speaking or smiling. Hermione closed the door behind him.

Bridie felt hopelessly confused and embarrassed. She had thought the hard part was over when she had got out of the car and rung the front door bell; now she saw it was only beginning. She thought – Oh God, why did I come? She went to the bay window, parted the curtains, and said, 'Can you see the sea front from here?'

Hermione didn't answer. She sat on the sofa beside the fire, knees spread beneath her full, tent-like robe. She had straight, cropped, dark grey hair, a strong, heavy face, red-rimmed, sharp eyes. She looked much, much older than Muff.

Bridie said, 'I suppose you can't, really, I mean, the road twists, doesn't it? But it would be nice, to look out on the sea.'

Hermione said, 'Why don't you sit down?'

Bridie sat, in a chair facing her mother. She tried to smile but her facial muscles seemed paralysed. She looked at the fire and spread out her hands to the flames. She said, 'How nice, to see a real fire! I stayed in a hotel the other day and I was quite taken in by one of those fake gas arrangements. Flames, and mock logs! Quite pretty to look at, and I suppose it is good for the tourist trade, so very Olde England! But I believe they are expensive to run. Although in an hotel, I suppose it saves labour costs.'

Hermione said, 'I know nothing about the economics of managing an hotel. It is a long time since I have stayed in one.'

'I'm sorry.'

'Why?'

'I don't know.'

Hermione sighed ostentatiously. 'I don't mind your coming to see me. As long as you are not expecting affection or money. Or alcohol, either. I can offer you tea or instant coffee, but no stronger drink, I'm afraid. If I keep a bottle in the house, my son in law finds it. When he gets drunk he either weeps or breaks the place up. I'm not sure which kind of behaviour is worse. It depends on how much damage he does, I suppose. This lunch time, he got drunk in a public house and smashed a number of glasses. He was trying to cut his veins, so he said, but we've all heard that sob story before. That's why the policeman was here. He came to tell me that Willie was safely tucked up in a cell for the night and sleeping it off. The local police are immensely considerate.'

She seemed perfectly calm about this situation.

Bridie said, 'Who's the boy?'

'My grandson. Willie and Cassie's son. Their only child, fortunately. Cassie is teaching in London. Willie was living with her until about ten months ago when he took a turn for the worse. He started turning up at the school, maudlin drunk, beating his breast and moaning on about what a useless sod he was, and how, if he had any decency, he'd put an end to himself. It is quite an affecting performance, the first time you observe it, and some of the children were upset as you can imagine. So I persuaded him to come here. Cassie needs a break, and I can manage him better than she can. And I'm quite fond of him. When sober, he is an agreeable companion, does a bit of typing and proof-reading for me, and we play Scrabble together sometimes after supper. Benedict is a boarder at a school outside Brighton. He goes to Cassie sometimes, when he has a free weekend, but mostly he comes to me. I usually return him on Sunday afternoon but tomorrow is some sort of Founder's Holiday. There is a school picnic, but Benedict prefers to stay here and read. He's a bookish boy, not very sociable. Anything else you want to know?'

'That seems to be quite enough to be going on with.' Bridie was surprised to hear herself speaking so tartly. An edge to her voice, like her mother's! Amused by this thought she said, boldly, 'I'm afraid I haven't read your books.'

'Why afraid? Plenty of other people in your plight, dearie!' Hermione cackled, red-rimmed eyes snapping and sparkling, displaying a neat row of small, pointed, yellow teeth. 'You're not such a little mouse, are you? Thank God for that! As a matter of fact, if you like, I *can* give you a drink. There should be a bottle of whisky on the top bookshelf. As far as I know, Willie's not found it! I hid it up there on my birthday, last July, thinking I might have a little nip to celebrate quietly if Willie went out. Unfortunately, when the chair broke beneath me, I twisted my ankle and I haven't cared to risk climbing up again. Old bones are brittle and I have what the social workers call a heavy case-load to carry! But if you'll get it down, it might cheer us both. The bookshelves on the right of the fireplace.'

Bridie fetched a hard chair from the window bay and looked at it carefully before she climbed on it.

'It's behind the *Dictionary of Historical Slang*,' Hermione said. 'You might get the dictionary down, while you're about it. I've needed it several times but I've been unable to ask Willie, for obvious reasons.'

Bridie brought the heavy book down and climbed up again for the whisky. Hermione rose, grunting, opened a cupboard and took out two tumblers. She poured them both a good measure.'

'Shall I put the bottle back?' Bridie asked.

'Oh, I daresay we'll kill it.'

They sat, facing each other. Bridie sipped her drink. It was a good malt, strong and velvety.

She said cautiously, 'Cassie is teaching in London. What about Matthew?'

'In America. He works with computers. He emigrated fourteen years ago, the first chance he got. Glad to get away. He had a bad time with his father. I don't know what Hilary's told you. He was a drunk, my dear husband. And nasty with it, not like poor Willie. Both my children had a rotten time when Gilbert came back from the war. Though there is no need to go into that. As you've said, you've heard enough to be going on with!' She gave her sharp, witch's cackle, drained her glass, and refilled it. 'You were luckier than they were. Or you could say, I suppose, that I did rather better for you! Being brought up by Hilary Mudd must be about the best start in life anyone could have!'

'Oh,' Bridie said. 'Well.' She laughed, feeling foolish. 'Yes, I suppose so.'

Hermione drank. She said, thoughtfully, 'You know if you were to put Hilary into a book, you would make her into a kind of leech, a terrible woman whose goodness destroys other people. Rebecca West wrote an excellent story about a woman like that. I can't remember the title now, but I remember I thought about Hilary the first time I read it. I was forced to conclude that Hilary didn't fit into that category. Her goodness is harmless. If she has a fault, it is that she cannot believe that anyone she cares for could be imperfect. I suppose that might be hard on her loved ones sometimes.'

'I love her very much indeed,' Bridie said sternly.

'So you should,' Hermione said, sounding surprised. 'My God, you would be the most awful little shit if you didn't. Have some more whisky.'

'No thank you,' Bridie said. Then she feared that this sounded prudish. 'I'm driving. And I had wine at lunch.' Hermione looked at her, grinning. 'Oh, all right,' Bridie said. 'Just a drop.'

She held out her glass. Hermione poured rather more than a drop into it. She sat back, cradling her own glass to her breast like a baby. She said, 'I loved Hilary almost the first time I met her. At our frightful school. It was a peculiar experience for me to find I could love someone so easily. I wasn't an affectionate girl. My parents were not affectionate people. Although they were quite adequately fond of me, and of each other, it was always decently hidden. But with Hilary there was no need to hide anything. No need for defences because *she* had none.'

Bridie said, 'She got into your bed the first night at school because you were crying and cold.'

'I don't remember that. I daresay it's true, if she told you.' She gave Bridie a lecherous grin. 'Two little girls in bed would be looked upon differently nowadays, wouldn't it? Enjoying a bit of a kiss and a cuddle! I expect I did fancy her, as they'd say now. Though it seemed innocent enough at the time.'

'I'm sure it was,' Bridie said, shocked. She thought – *I am dreaming this*! Sitting here with this dreadful old woman, drinking her whisky . . .

She put her glass down. She said, 'I ought to go, really.'

'Why?' Hermione felt in the pocket of her capacious gown and produced a packet of small cigars and a box of matches. She lit a cigar and stretched out her long, pretty feet to the fire. She said, 'There must be a few things we have to say to each other. Or that you want to say to me. You must have come for some reason.'

'Idle curiosity,' Bridie said, stung by her calm, amused tone.

'A bit more than that, perhaps, but not *much*.' She stopped, ashamed. Why was she being so rude? After all, she was the intruder here! She said, 'I suppose I simply felt that I wanted to see you. Not just for myself, but for Pansy, too. For my daughter.'

She waited for Hermione to respond to this. She must feel some interest, surely? In her own grand-daughter? Even if she didn't, she ought to pretend she did, Bridie decided indignantly. It was, simply, good manners!

She said, 'Pansy is a remarkable child in many ways. Independent, and pretty, and clever. A strong girl, a strong *person*, very sensible, very practical.'

'I'm delighted to hear it,' Hermione said. She smoked and coughed drily.

Bridie said, 'I don't think she *worries*, exactly, but one never really knows, does one? She must wonder, sometimes. After all, she knows that I was adopted, and there might come a day . . . I could at least tell her I'd *seen* you!'

Hermione coughed again, jerking her glass and spilling her whisky. She dabbed at the drops on her breast with the sleeve of her dress and threw her half-smoked cigar into the fire. She said, 'Your marriage has broken up, hasn't it? Martin told me. He said it had thrown you off course. Those are the words that he used. That's why you're here, isn't it? So why don't you say so? Instead of this pretence about Pansy who is a lucky girl by the sound of it. Plenty of parental and grand-parental concern all about her.'

'It's a matter of *knowing*,' Bridie said. 'Not affection – you're quite right to say Pansy doesn't need that, any more than I do – but straight information. It might help her to establish herself, know who she is, if she knows where she comes from, what sort of people. What her grandfather was like, for example!'

Hermione stared at her blankly and Bridie was furious with herself. It had been dishonest and stupid to put her question in that oblique way. Cowardly, too. Rather as if she had gone to a doctor with a disease she was ashamed to admit to and asked for advice about a 'friend's problem.' She smiled apologetically and said, 'Though of course, if you don't want to talk about him, I do understand. I mean, if it's painful, and I can see that it could be, even now, after all this time. My mother – that is, your friend Hilary – told me all that she knew about him, which wasn't much, really. Just that he was a pleasant young man who had once kindly mended her bicycle, and that he never knew you were pregnant. She said you were terribly brave, going off as you did without telling him, especially when you loved him so much.'

'Who on earth are you talking about?' Hermione asked.

Bridie looked at the heavy old woman, at the tired, handsome old face and the bloodshot eyes that were staring so strangely – not blankly now, but with a kind of stunned, bewildered amazement – and felt pity for her. Poor thing, she was so old and so weary, and it was so long ago, that lost love . . .

She said, speaking softly and gently. 'Perhaps it's wrong to have asked you about him. To bring it all back. But I'm talking about my *father*, of course! The Italian. *Mario*! That was his name, wasn't it? Now I think of it, I suppose that's why my parents christened me Mary!' That would be like Muff, she thought. Naming her adopted child after the father she would never know, preserving this sweet link between them! She said, blinking back tears, 'I mean, I really have only just thought of that!'

Hermione laughed. She put her glass down on the floor and roared – a huge belly laugh, shaking her mountainous frame.

'Oh my God,' she gasped. 'Oh, my dear Christ, I'd forgotten! That romantic old rubbish I told her! Riding what Rebecca West once called the tosh horse! I never thought it would stick. Oh, my dear Lord! I should have known Martin would never have had the guts to own up. What a *bloody* man he is, really!'

'I don't understand you,' Bridie said. Although the room was warm, she had started to shiver; beads of cold sweat breaking out on her forehead. She thought – oh, of course, she's a lush, why didn't I see it before? Going on about her alcoholic son in law when *she's* a drunk, too. Hiding whisky bottles in bookshelves, lying about twisting her ankle and being unable to reach it!

Hermione said, 'Have another drink. It'll steady you. It would steady me, too. Would you mind?'

Bridie got up from her chair, picked up Hermione's glass from the floor and poured generously. Hermione gulped at her drink and shuddered a little. Bridie sat down, watching her fearfully. The old woman's eyes glinted with angry amusement.

'He should have told you. Or at least have warned me! Well, it's out now. A shock for you. I should say, I suppose, that I'm sorry. Your father's a fool. Not that I blame him too much. I can see the fix he was in. *I* didn't have the courage to tell her, so why should I expect *him* to? How could either of us have told that innocent creature?' She lit another cigar, drew on it, and looked at Bridie with, for the first time, some animosity.

'Listen!' she said. 'There was Hilary. My best, my only *real* friend, who had always been good to me. We were living in the country, two still fairly young women, sitting out the war with our children. I was bored to tears. I didn't much care for my husband, Gilbert was a brute and a bully, but at least our life had been *lively*. Stuck there on that bloody farm, nothing to do except trot round with the kids, amusing them, shovelling food into them, walking miles to the shops. No fun, no parties, no sex – that bothered me, I can tell you. I had been used to a regular ration. At least Hilary had Martin occasionally. And she loved her dotty old aunt and her daughter. Then they died, one after the other. Even Hilary almost went under. Oh, she didn't give way. She was like a piece of frozen ground. She didn't cry at her child's funeral. She stood there, watching the earth thud down on that sad little coffin, with that controlled, frozen face. Such contained, *private* grief. No one could share it. She went straight home, nursed her aunt. She had such strength. More than Martin. He needed comfort. I provided it. That was all.'

'All?' Absurdly, to her horror, Bridie found herself wanting to laugh. Her voice tumbled with this shocking laughter. She said, 'Oh, poor Muff!'

Hermione said, with interest, 'Is that what you call her?'

Bridie nodded, ashamed. Admitting this childish nickname seemed a kind of betrayal.

'I did my best,' Hermione said. 'I cut and run. I hadn't told Martin I was pregnant, I didn't tell Hilary where I was going. I hoped neither of them would ever know. It was my one thought, and, to be fair to myself, a quite decent one. I didn't think beyond it. I dumped the kids. I *hoped* – well, we won't go into that. In the circumstances it hardly seems fair to you. And, in any event, I had neither the courage nor the money to try anything beyond gin and hot baths. But then *she* turned up. My best friend, my saviour, coming to look after me, taking me under her wing, an angel of mercy and charity! What could I do?'

She smiled, grimly at first, then broke into a sharp, gleeful cackle. 'You could say, I suppose, that it was the beginning of my career! That story about the Italian prisoner! The situation I found myself in was the kind to concentrate the mind wonderfully. I couldn't just tell Hilary this good tale and leave it at that. She wasn't a fool. I had to convince her. Putting bones on the flesh of the first lie I thought of, I discovered I had quite a nice little talent! And it came in remarkably useful when old Gilbert came back from the war. Kept him and the kids, paid for their education and his liquor bills.' She looked at Bridie and lifted her glass. 'All your doing, you might say! We should all be grateful.'

'Don't be so bloody arch.'

Hermione raised her eyebrows and grinned.

'You're *enjoying* yourself,' Bridie said angrily.

'Do you really think that I shouldn't? Oh, for Christ's sake, girl, don't start to be prissy. This is all ancient history.'

'Not for me.'

'That's not my fault, is it?'

'No. Perhaps not.' Bridie thought – I should be angry with

Dadda! But she didn't feel angry with him. She felt protective and sorry. How terrified he must have been when she burst in upon him with her impetuous questions! How scared he must be *now*, that she would find out, tell Muff. After all these years it would be such a dreadful betrayal. Not even Muff could forgive him for making such a farce of their happy life, their good marriage, her joy in their adopted daughter! She said, miserably, 'He ought to have told me.'

'I daresay he couldn't get his tongue round it. Or perhaps he just hoped that nothing would happen. That would be like him.' Hermione laughed, baring her small, yellow teeth. 'When we got to London, Hilary wrote to him, naturally, about my predicament. Told him the tale I'd told *her* – before she wrote, she actually asked my permission? You'd have thought it might have crossed his mind that I'd made it all up, that I'd lied in order to spare him! But apparently not. It seemed that he believed what Hilary told him . . .'

Her cigar had gone out. She looked at the butt as if wondering whether to light it again, then muttered under her breath, 'Filthy habit, you disgusting old woman, you don't even enjoy it, why don't you stop it?' and threw it into the grate. She said, 'I think – it's hard to remember now, but I *think*, if he'd asked me, when he came to the hospital – I might have stuck to my story. I could have told him that what I'd told Hilary was quite true. That I'd been having it off with my young Italian before Gracie died, and that I was already pregnant when Martin and I hit the hay. It would have been credible! We'd only done it a couple of times, after all! But he stood at the end of my bed, poker-stiff, keeping his distance, as if there had never been anything between us at all, not so much as a fumble, and it got my goat, rather! There I was, handing my baby over, making amends to my friend, as I thought – she was so *hungry* for you, I'd seen it in her face when she held you – and there *he* was, getting away with it, behaving for all the world as if he were doing me a great favour.'

'Well he was, wasn't he?' Bridie said crossly.

'Not exactly, my dear! They could just have taken you, without a formal adoption. No questions, no trouble! But Martin insisted that it should all be done properly – for your sake, he said, and that, as he knew perfectly well, was no favour to me! As the law stood at that time, if a married woman wanted to dispose of a baby, a little wartime mistake, her husband had to sign the adoption papers. Gilbert had to sign them when he came home. And that meant more lying, of course. What I told *him*, was that my child's father had been an American soldier, that I'd gone to a dance at an American base camp and got drunk and didn't even know the man's name. More practice in my craft, possibly, but it didn't exactly make for peace in the home. On the other hand, it gave Gilbert a royal grievance against me, and he needed that badly. Those years in the prison camp had broken him up, he couldn't hold down a job, and after a bit, he couldn't get one. I was beginning to be successful, if only in a small way, and his life was over. Having something to hurl at me when he was drunk eased him considerably.'

Bridie gazed into the fire. What shocked her most, she decided, was the cool, reflective way her mother had told her all this. As if it were *normal* for life to be such a tangled network of lies and deceit! Of course, as she'd said, it was an old tale to her. She was looking back, all passion spent. A sad, tired old woman at the end of her life . . .

She said, 'It must have been dreadful for you. I'm sorry.'

She looked at Hermione and saw she was yawning. Yawning and smiling. She said, 'Oh, I managed, you know. It gave me something to get my teeth into. Some people thrive on adversity. I fear that I'm one of them.'

Bridie said, tentatively, 'You enjoy your work, don't you? Your writing?'

'Most of the time. Though there is no worse tyranny than a job you enjoy. I sometimes wish that I'd chosen a nine-to-five job. But of course, if I *had*, I'd have been on the scrap-heap at my age. A pensioner, an old has-been!' She chortled, as if the idea of her being old was enormously funny. 'What are you going to do? Now that you're off on your own?'

'I don't know. Get a job. Nine-to-five, as you say. I haven't really tried yet. I suppose I've been taking stock first.' Bridie laughed, a little self-consciously. 'Trying to get myself straight before I get started again. All I really know how to do is to run a house, cook, and look after people. I rushed into marrying James, when I was only nineteen, without thinking. . . .'

'Don't tell me about it,' Hermione said. She picked up the whisky bottle, held it up to examine the level, then emptied it, a little into Bridie's glass, a rather larger amount into her own. She went on, in a gentler voice, 'I really don't want to *know*, d'you see? I haven't the interest to spare. I've got Willie and the boy to look after and my work to get done. That takes all my energy. I'm sorry if it sounds brutal. I'm glad you escaped from your marriage, if that's what you wanted.'

'Why didn't you escape?' Bridie smiled cheerfully to show that she wasn't hurt by this dismissal. 'After all, you could have done, couldn't you? You were earning a living. You could have brought up Cassie and Matthew, sent Gilbert packing.'

'Well, you put your hand to the plough,' Hermoine said. 'As one of our schoolmistresses used to say. Hilary will remember her name, I expect – we both had what we used to call "a bit of a pash" on her. And there were the children. Matthew hated Gilbert. No, that's too strong. He disliked and despised him and kept out of his way as much as he could. But Cassie was fond of him. Sometimes I think that was why she got married to Willie. He reminded her of her father. You know, if you ever felt like it, she might be quite pleased to see you. She was always curious.'

'Do you mean, she *knew* about me? Did you actually tell her?'

'Gilbert told her. He used to go and sit on her bed, some nights when he came home sorrowful drunk, and mourn over what he called her 'lost little sister.' In rather vague terms to begin with. Later on he became more specific. Only another stick to beat *me* with, but as she grew up, Cassie chose to see it as an excuse for Gilbert's unhappy condition. Gilbert was a romantic figure to her; the silly girl was attracted by failure. And was glad to blame me, since we'd never got on well together. If only I hadn't *let her father down* in the war, and so on, and so forth . . .'

She fell silent, eyes half-closed, heavy face brooding. Bridie watched her, too dazed and bewildered to speak. This old woman and her daughter – her *mother*, she reminded herself, her *half-sister* – had known all about her, even quarrelled because of her, and she had not even known they existed! It should be a deeply sentimental and moving discovery, Bridie thought, but in fact she felt only slightly uncomfortable – rather as if she had suddenly found out that some of her neighbours in Westbridge or Islington, people she neither knew very well, nor cared much about, had been gossiping about her behind her back.

Eventually, Hermione got up from her chair and went to a desk in the corner of the room. She sat on the swivel chair, switched on the Anglepoise lamp, opened a drawer and began rifling through it. It occurred to Bridie that she was almost certainly looking for something to give her as a memento. A book, a photograph, even, perhaps, a piece of old family jewellery. Well, of course, it would be the obvious, conventional thing to do in this situation (though she wouldn't have thought Hermione was the sort to do the obvious, conventional thing!) and she must try to respond in the same spirit. Sitting stiff and straight in her chair, smiling pleasantly, Bridie determined that whatever Hermione produced, however little she wanted it, she would do her best to accept it gracefully.

Hermione twisted round on her chair and held out a small piece of paper. She said, 'Cassie's telephone number. Ring her up if you feel like it.'

Bridie got up. Although she was conscious of a faint disappointment, she continued to smile as she took the paper and put it into her purse. She said, 'Thank you.' Then added, uneasily, 'Would you like me to come and see you again?'

Hermione blinked. The light from the Anglepoise lamp fell full on her face and Bridie saw that in spite of the red, veiny whites, her eyes were a beautiful colour; a pale, golden brown, like clear tea. Bridie said, 'If I could help in any way, I'd be glad to.'

Hermione looked at her. 'It's up to you. I can hardly prevent you. But if you want my opinion, I think this has been the most interesting conversation we are ever likely to have. If we tried to follow it up, I fear we would find we had very little to say to each other.' She looked at the watch on her wrist. 'I don't want to appear inhospitable, but we have finished the whisky, and it's time for Benedict's supper.' She clapped her hands on her knees and stood up; as she crossed the room, the floor shook beneath her.

They went into the hall. Hermione opened the front door. On the doorstep, Bridie turned and said, in a panic, 'I'm sorry. There's one thing. Do you often speak to my father?'

'Christ, *no*! How old are you?'

'Thirty-two.'

'Then I haven't spoken to your father for thirty-two years.'

'Oh. I see. I just wondered. You did say, when I came, that he'd warned you.'

'He wrote. Through my publishers. I didn't write back.' Hermione yawned and scratched herself under one breast. Then she looked at her watch again.

Bridie said, 'Look. Just a minute. I'm sorry to keep you, but it *is* difficult, isn't it? I mean, in a way, it seems so dishonest. But it could be so painful for him. If he even guessed that I'd been here! Wondering, waiting, for me to say something. He's kept quiet all these years and I can see that he had to. If he'd told Muff before – I mean, told her that he'd been unfaithful with you *before* he knew you were pregnant, it would have been awful, of course, for them both, but somehow more bearable. But if he believed, or half-believed, anyway, what she'd written and told him about this Italian, by the time he came to the hospital and heard the truth from you, it was already too late. He was *caught*! It would have been too cruel to tell her at that point! And, with each passing year, it must have got harder. Although I expect it's become part of his life, sort of woven into the fabric, not hidden, exactly, but something he's learned how to live with, to bring it out in the open *now* might be terrible . . .'

'I promise you that I won't write and tell him,' Hermione said.

'Thank you,' Bridie said. She laughed. 'It seems dreadful.'

'Only if you choose to tie yourself up in knots over it.'

'You can't pretend that there isn't a problem.'

Hermione shrugged and smiled slightly. There was a cold, amused light in her eyes.

Bridie said, in what she hoped was a calm and dignified manner, 'My problem, not yours, of course. I accept that. But it seems only sensible that you should know what I think I intend to do about it. Even if sometime or other I can see that he knows, in his heart, that *I* know, I shall probably keep quiet about it.'

Hermione's smile broadened into a wide grin of delight. Bridie blushed. 'You're your father's daughter, all right,' Hermione said, and closed the door on her.

Chapter Eight

'You're early,' Martin Mudd said, as he opened the door of the flat. 'The plane isn't due to land till eleven.'

He was still in his dressing-gown. Bridie followed him into the kitchen where he was preparing Muff's breakfast tray.

'I thought Aunt Florence might be fussing,' she said. 'Traffic, and so on. And the weather is filthy! Rain and wind. Squally.'

'It's nine fifteen now. If you leave here at ten o'clock you will be in plenty of time. Florence has had breakfast and she's dressing now. Do you want coffee?'

'No, thank you, Dadda. I'll have a cup of tea with Muff.'

'Anything to eat? I can easily put on another egg. Or make toast.'

'Just the tea.'

'Sure?'

'Quite sure, Dadda.'

The innocent normality of this exchange was consoling to Bridie who had spent most of the twenty-four hours since she drove back from Brighton conducting a series of imaginary conversations with her father on a much more emotional level. Now, sitting in her parents' warm kitchen, watching him cut Muff's thin bread and butter while her egg chattered away on the stove, she realised with relief that none of those conversations were likely to take place in reality. And, for her own comfort, the fact that they had taken place in her mind was sufficient. Muttering to herself as she walked along the canal bank (for hours, in the pouring rain) she had reproached him, forgiven him, and finally felt her love for him stretch like a flexible skin to contain her new knowledge. Like a balloon, she thought fancifully – and reminded herself that balloons were easily punctured. One prick from a foolish word and the whole of their lives would burst open!

She said, 'It really is the most horrible weather this morning.' She shrugged up her shoulders and affected to shiver.

'So you just said. What do you expect in November? But Blodwen's flight is on time. I rang the airport a few minutes ago. She's coming in at Terminal Two. She was flying on a jumbo from Sydney to Amsterdam, then changing to KLM for some reason.'

'How is Aunt Florence bearing up?'

'She was in a bit of a state yesterday evening. Said she couldn't face Blodwen. But I gave her a sleeping pill and she's fairly steady this morning. Ready to march towards the sound of the guns without flinching. Muff is tired, though.'

'I'm sorry.'

He put the bread and butter on a plate, neatly fanning the slices, took the egg from the saucepan, put it in its egg cup and covered it with the small red cosy that Bridie had embroidered for Muff years ago. He said, 'I gather she told you what you wanted to know. What we talked about the last time I saw you.' He gave a sharp laugh and glanced at her. 'I trust that you're satisfied.' He poured boiling water into the teapot and grumbled, 'Upsetting your mother!'

Bridie hoped the terror that seized her did not show in her face. 'I don't think Muff was upset.'

'Hmm. Well. Maybe not. She wouldn't let you know if she was, of course. Did it make any difference to you? Or whatever you wanted?'

'Not really, Dadda.'

Ah, but it had, she thought. Seeing Hermione, that tough,

coarse old woman, she had seen where her own coarseness came from. And was not ashamed of it any longer. It could be a source of strength, as it seemed to be in this situation. A truly sensitive, nice-minded woman would have been shattered! But although the consciously thinking part of herself was certainly shocked by her father's deceit, deep down, in the subterranean caverns of her mind, laughter was rumbling. She knew her father better now, and, understanding him, seeing how he had got himself into this fix, she felt she had grown larger and wiser. She could never be purely good and gentle like Muff, but she could be strong, like her gallant old mother!

Martin was watching her. 'There's an end to it, then?'

'Yes.'

'Good.'

The firm pads of flesh on his cheekbones were fiery red. *The old hypocrite*, she thought, lovingly, tenderly, *the splendid, wicked, old humbug!* Hugging his secret! Well, as far as she was concerned, he could take it to the grave with him. But what a chance he had taken! If Hermione had ever turned nasty! Perhaps that was unlikely. But even if he had had nothing to fear from Hermione, he must surely have had something to fear from himself? He and Muff were so close; husband and wife, friends and lovers. The desire to confess must have been so strong sometimes . . .

Martin said, 'No point in raking over dead ashes. We've had enough of that sort of palaver these last few days with old Florence. I hope she behaves herself at the airport. She and Blodwen will just have to shake down together somehow. I'll do what I can to keep peace between them but it's Muff I must think of. You take her tray, she's been looking forward to seeing you. I'll go and shave, if Florence is out of the bathroom.'

Florence said, 'She won't make old bones, your poor mother, will she?'

'Muff is stronger than she looks,' Bridie said. Her aunt was only making conversation, she told herself. Blodwen's plane had landed twenty minutes ago and Florence was growing visibly and painfully nervous, rattling her coffee cup as she put it down on the saucer, and dabbing fretfully at the thin line of her lips with her handkerchief.

'Well, it's worn out I thought she was looking last night,' Florence continued. 'Martin should take better care of her.'

'He does his best,' Bridie said. 'I didn't think she seemed too bad this morning. She said she'd had a good night.'

'Oh, she'd put on a good front for you, I daresay,' Florence said disapprovingly. 'Old people don't like to let themselves down in front of their children. And you've been seeing her regularly, so you won't have noticed the change in her. But to my mind, she's gone down a lot since last Easter.'

Bridie choked back a giggle. She saw now why her aunt had brought up this topic! To make sure that Bridie would back up her story about the new bed! Oh, the cunning old creature! 'Was that when they came down to stay with you?' Bridie asked, smiling innocently.

Florence didn't answer. As she touched the cameo brooch at the neck of her blouse, Bridie saw that her fingers were trembling. She had dressed to meet Blodwen as if for a wedding: a cream-coloured, wool coat, matching kid gloves, a pink, frilly blouse. Above these pale, festive garments, her small, shrunken face looked like a dark, pickled walnut.

She said, 'I told Martin. If you want Hilary to see the next spring, you should take her away. Out of this damp old country into the sun. The Algarve, or North Africa. I wouldn't go out of England myself, wasting my good money on foreigners, but *he* can afford it.' She looked round the airport terminal and said, in a quite different voice, with a sudden, shy catch of breath, 'Why is Blod being so long?'

'She'll be here soon. We can go and wait at the gate, if you like.' Florence gave a small, gasping moan. Her mouth was twitching with panic. Bridie said, to distract her, 'It's not as if she were coming in on the jumbo. They take simply ages to get through immigration and customs. But she's coming from

Amsterdam on this KLM flight. Though she flew to Amsterdam on the jumbo.'

Florence controlled herself, pursed her lips angrily. 'How she could, I don't know! All that way! You wouldn't get me on one of those nasty great planes, not for a thousand pounds, I can tell you! Think if it crashed, all those people!' She touched her brooch again, like a talisman. 'I'm surprised at Blodwen! She was always so very particular!'

Bridie frowned at this obscure remark, then understood it. 'Darling Aunt Florence, if you die, it can hardly matter how many other people die with you. But she's quite safe, she's landed! Honestly, it's up on the board. She really will be through the gate any minute.'

She stood up. Florence got up from her chair very slowly, wincing as she bent to pick up her bag, her umbrella. She said, 'I'll go and meet her. You get the car. She won't want to hang about after that terrible journey.' Her face was a dull, uniform red; set like stone. She looked sternly at Bridie. 'Go along now. What are you waiting for? I don't need a nursemaid. Do you think I'm not capable of recognising my own sister?'

Bridie fled. There was a solid lump in her throat and a mixture of rain and tears blinded her eyes as she ran across the access road outside the terminal, dodging hooting buses and cabs, to get to the car-park. How sentimental, she thought, as she pressed the bell for the lift, how *utterly silly*! But her chest was heaving like bellows and by the time the lift came, she was weeping luxuriously.

The grey metal doors opened. Which level had she left the car on? She couldn't remember. She entered the lift and pressed the top button. 'Start at the top and work down, you incompetent oaf,' she said aloud, between sobs, and then realised that she wasn't alone. Someone had pushed his way into the lift at the last moment; the doors had almost closed on him.

Philip said, 'Bridie!' He was breathing hard. 'Didn't you *hear* me? I shouted and shouted! Do you know, you were nearly knocked down, crossing that road, you weren't *looking* . . . What on earth is the matter?'

'N-nothing.' She turned her face away – she must look so awful, puffy and blubbery – but he caught her chin with his fingers and forced her to look at him. She smiled at him shakily, relieved to see that he wasn't wearing his glasses, then said, fresh tears falling, 'I m-mean, nothing serious. J-just my old aunt. She's meeting her sister from Australia, they've not *seen* each other for, I don't know, something *incredible* like f-fifty years. And my aunt, the one *I* know, that is, the one who lives here, who I brought to the airport, was being so angry and frightened. They'd had this great row, you see, years ago, and – oh, it's no good, it would take too long to explain. But it seemed so sad, somehow.'

Philip was laughing. He said, 'Oh, you darling.'

'Though I expect, the moment they meet, they'll start quarrelling.'

The lift had stopped on the top floor. The automatic doors opened. They went through them, into a howling gale that tugged at their clothing. Philip put his arm round her. She said, 'I remember now. I left the car on the third floor. How stupid. I'm sorry.'

The lift had departed. Philip pressed the bell to recall it.

Bridie said, 'Where's your car? The Saab?'

Philip pointed. 'On the other side of that pillar. You can see her snubby green nose poking out.'

'Well, then. Hadn't you better . . . ?'

'No. I don't think so. I'll come with you first. You might forget again, otherwise. I mean, you lose your way rather easily, don't you?' He fished his glasses out of his pocket, put them on, and looked at her through them. She widened her hot eyes, hoping that they didn't look as red as they felt, and pulled the top of her scalp back to smooth out her forehead. He said, 'Do you know your licence number?'

'Of course I do. It's . . . Well . . .' She covered her mouth and nose with her hand and laughed at him over it. He smiled at her, raising his eyebrows. She said, 'I'm sure I do know it, really.'

His smile broadened. He said, 'I wasn't trying to be condescending and sexist. I couldn't tell you mine, either. Not just off the cuff, anyway. It's nice to meet someone else who has no memory for that sort of thing. Though it's funny, I can always remember telephone numbers!'

The lift had returned. The doors opened. They walked into the lift and Philip pressed the bell. He said, 'I was going to ring you this evening.'

'Why didn't you . . .?' She laughed. 'I mean, why this evening, particularly?' He looked at her as the lift lurched rustily downwards. She said, 'I mean, why not before?'

'I did. I rang on Sunday, from Shropshire. But there was no answer.'

'I was in Brighton.'

'Oh. That would explain it, then.'

She laughed again. For some reason this response seemed amazingly witty.

He said, 'The reason I didn't ring you before was because I had something to finish.' He paused, then went on, rather more rapidly, 'There was a girl I was sort of, well, living with. Off and on, only more off than on, latterly.'

The lift juddered and stopped but the doors remained closed. 'Jammed between floors,' Philip said. 'How odd, to find a mechanical contrivance that behaves so obligingly.'

She thought he meant he was going to kiss her but he made no move towards her. They were standing apart, almost the whole width of the lift between them.

He said, 'What I just said, I suppose it must have sounded like a declaration of some kind. I suppose I meant it that way. Well, yes, I did, actually. But please ignore it, if you prefer to.'

She stared at him. A young man with clear, healthy blue eyes, a slightly freckled, fair skin. His blonde hair was silky, his mouth smooth and firm. He was both an old friend and a stranger. She looked at his smooth mouth and shivered.

He said, in an accusing voice, 'I wouldn't have said that if you hadn't been crying.'

Somewhere below them there was a sound of shouting and thumping. The lift started to move again and stopped with a jerk. The doors opened at the third floor. Two extremely large men in dark overcoats pushed their way in and, at once, the doors closed behind them.

Philip and Bridie looked at each other and grinned. The lift descended to the ground floor. The two large men left. The doors remained open. Philip said, 'If you like, we could use the stairs. It might be quicker in the end.'

Bridie said, 'I've become quite attached to this lift.' She pushed the bell. 'Though I ought to hurry up, really. My aunt, my *aunts*, will be waiting. Do you really remember my telephone number?'

He repeated it. She loooked at him admiringly. She smiled, to encourage him. But he seemed speechless.

She said, 'I could cry again, if it helps.'

His cheeks coloured. 'No. No, there's no need for that. Unless you feel like it. Look. Are you by any chance free tomorrow evening? There's a good place I know, a little French dining club in Clink Street. Off Shaftsbury Avenue. You can't miss it, there's only one restaurant. The Clink Club. They have good food and the best cheese in London. Do you like cheese?'

'Yes.'

'Good. Well, more than good. *Splendid*. Could you come, say, about seven thirty?'

She nodded. 'Thank you. I'd love to.'

The lift stopped. The doors opened. He took her arm and hurried her through them. 'Success!' He beamed at her. 'Now, do you know where your car is?'

'On the right somewhere.'

They walked between lines of parked cars. He kept hold of her arm. She could feel the warmth of his hand through the sleeve of her coat. He said, 'We could make it tonight, of course, only I expect you'll be busy. If this aunt of yours has just arrived from Australia. I imagine that means some sort of welcoming party?'

She was astonished to find him so thoughtful. So immensely considerate. She remembered that he understood about families.

She said, 'My parents will expect me to dinner. These two aunts, they're my father's sisters. What they quarrelled about, was the husband of the Australian one. My Aunt Blodwen. She went off with Aunt Florence's boy friend. She married him and they emigrated. He's dead now, he died years ago, but Aunt Blodwen never wrote to Aunt Florence to tell her. So until very recently, when my father told her, Florence thought he was coming to England with Blodwen. She had even bought a new double bed for them, for Blodwen and Harry. New sheets and blankets and everything. So she was naturally furious, all the expense that she'd gone to. Though of course it was really that she felt such a fool!' She giggled. 'I don't know why I am telling you all this. It's so ludicrous.'

'I wouldn't say so. It sounds fascinating. I shall be interested to hear how the situation develops.'

'I can tell you tomorrow. At the Clink Club.'

'Yes. Yes, *please*!'

They had reached the Renault. He was holding her left arm, his hand under her elbow. He continued to hold it while she fished her keys out of her pocket and opened the car door. Then he let her go and stood back.

She started the engine, leaving the door open in case he intended to lean in and kiss her. She would be pleased if he did, she thought, but she wouldn't be hurt if he didn't. She waited a moment, revving the engine in neutral, then solved the prob-lem by kissing the tips of her fingers and waving them in his direction before slamming the door and putting the car into gear. He responded with a smile – a *lovely* smile, she thought dizzily, feeling the blood pumping up in her cheeks and an extraordinary happiness swelling her chest and filling her lungs with deep, sighing breath. She backed the car and swung the wheel sharply, grazing the rear door of the adjacent car, a large Bentley, with her front bumper. She pulled a wry face at Philip, put the Renault into first gear and drove off, watching him in her mirror. He was standing still, looking after her; both arms raised above his head in farewell, and laughing . . .

It seemed to Bridie, looking round the dinner table at her family, at Muff and Dadda and Florence and Blodwen, that a kind of rosy enchantment hung over the evening. Perhaps the happiness she was feeling, which was a kind of glow, like perfect health, had affected the others in some mysterious way. They were all behaving so well − like good children, she thought, beaming at their elderly faces, flattered by candle light, animated by enjoyable memories of long ago family scandals. Great-uncle Horace Mudd, who had walked out of his house early one morning, wearing his working clothes, leaving a wife and five children, and had never been seen or heard of again; great-grandfather Ebenezer, an elder of his Welsh chapel, who had got a girl pregnant in his eighty-sixth year; Jasmine Mudd, their father's mother's third cousin, who had fed her husband all his life on tinned sardines and potatoes; Aunt Anne, who had gone mad at a wedding, torn her clothes off and danced on the table stark naked and who had, after the wedding, been 'put away.'

There was an advantage, Bridie perceived, in having a large extended family, and excellent memories. All these people under discussion were not only very distant relations, but also quite safely and comfortably *dead*: her father and his sisters could tear them to shreds without coming too close to home.

'It wasn't Aunt Anne who went mad,' Blodwen said. 'It was Milly.'

'Mother's Aunt Milly?' Florence touched her cameo brooch and jutted her jaw. 'Surely not, Blod? Mother always said that strain ran in Dad's family!'

'Oh, she would say that, wouldn't she?'

Blodwen's Australian accent had grown less pronounced as

the evening progressed; with this last sentence a clear Welsh lilt had crept back. Even her physical appearance seemed to have altered, Bridie thought, watching her. When she had seen her aunt first, at the airport, she had looked a stranger; a handsome, strong, rosy-faced woman in late middle age. Now, seeing her beside Florence and Martin, the family resemblance was marked. And not just the physical features; the neat head, the small, hawkish nose, the thick, wiry hair. There was a certain *look* that was evident on Blodwen's face at this moment, the way she was flaring her nostrils and turning the corners of her mouth down, that was familiar suddenly. Did *she* do that, Bridie wondered. After all, Aunt Florence had said (without thinking, of course!) that she looked like Aunt Blodwen! She glanced at her father. What would he say, how would he behave, if she asked Florence now if she still thought they looked like each other? Bridie had a curious, wild impulse to speak, ask this dangerous question, although, at the same time, her mouth dried with fear. . . .

Blodwen said, 'It was Mother's habit to disown that kind of thing, wasn't it? Blame our Dad for any little peculiarity, any family misfortune she didn't care to acknowledge?'

She laughed merrily – apparently ignorant, it seemed to Bridie, of the fuse she was lighting. Of course, Blodwen had been away from her brother and sister for such a long time, she might have forgotten how easy it was to provoke an explosion! But she must remember that she had left Florence to care for their mother! Walked out with Harry, *escaped* – leaving her older sister to carry the burden! Blodwen must know that, in Florence's view, her defection meant that she had no right to make this kind of criticism. Perhaps Blodwen didn't care, Bridie thought. Or perhaps she had simply grown bored with this unusually amiable evening and wanted a bit of excitement. Bridie was conscious that she felt a little excited herself at the prospect of a lively exchange between the two sisters. She looked at her father and saw he was grinning. He caught her eye and winked slyly.

Florence said, hissing ominously, 'I am surprised, Blodwen, that you can remember our Mother so clearly.'

Muff said, 'Would anyone like some more lamb? There is plenty, and roast lamb is so much nicer when it's hot, I always think. Not like beef, which is just as good cold.'

'No thank you, dear,' Blodwen said. 'That was a perfect meal. Beaut!' She turned to Florence and smiled; a sweet smile that seemed quite without guile. 'You were wonderful to Mother, Flo. The last time she wrote to me, her last letter, she said she was so grateful to you for your goodness and kindness. An angel, she said, to a crabby old woman.'

Florence sniffed. Although she didn't smile back, and all she said was, 'I did my duty, I hope,' it was clear that the danger had passed.

Muff rose from the table with a small, relieved sigh. Bridie helped her carry out dishes. She said, in the kitchen, 'I thought we were in for a flare-up.'

'Oh, that will come sooner or later,' Muff said. 'They can't do without it, that lot, it's meat and strong drink to them. I only hope they'll wait till they're out of my house.'

'Dadda says, Aunt Blodwen was always the spiteful one. But she doesn't seem to be, does she?'

'Biding her time, I expect,' Muff said serenely.

'She might have changed. All those years in Australia. Perhaps Harry was a good influence.'

Ssh. Don't mention his name, dear.' Hilary Mudd put her finger to her lips and looked mischievous. 'Don't you believe it! Leopards don't change their spots. You can smile and smile and still be a villain, you know! All that sweetness and light is just to disarm poor Florence. Put her off her guard and make it easier for Blodwen to stick the knife in, later on.'

Bridie giggled. 'Oh Muff, you are awful!'

'Long experience has taught me, my darling,' Muff said. 'I daresay when the others come — Blanche is arriving on Thursday and Sam on Friday — we shall see the fur fly. Luckily, the flat is too small to put them all up, Blanche and Sam are staying at the hotel round the corner. Could you reach down those pudding plates, dear? The ones on the top shelf. The best ones, the Crown Derby. They'll be a bit dusty, we don't often use them, but it won't take a minute to wipe them and we might as well kill the fatted calf properly while we're about it.'

Bridie climbed on the kitchen steps and passed these precious plates carefully, one by one, down to her mother.

She felt so relieved, she thought. Once or twice, in the course of this evening, she had found herself wondering, fearfully, if perhaps Muff had known all along about her 'best friend' and Dadda, and kept silent, to spare him. Not she realised that this was impossible. If Muff knew that her daughter was really, by blood, one of that family, she would never have spoken about them in that tart, amused way . . .

Then Muff said, 'I've made Floating Islands for pudding. You know, Pansy's favourite,' and Bridie saw that her mother's happiness was as fragile as the plates she was handling. Her own daughter's face rose up before her, smiling as Blodwen had smiled, with that prim, turned-down mouth, the faint flare of the nostrils.

'Are you all right, dear?' Muff took the last plate and regarded her anxiously. 'You've gone white as a sheet.' She put out a hand to help Bridie down.

Bridie laughed. 'Have I? I'm sorry.'

'Is it your period, dear?'

'No. I just felt a bit giddy. It's gone now. I don't know what it was. Stupid!'

Stupid was right, she told herself. There was no objective, discernible likeness between Blodwen and Pansy. It was only guilt that had made her look for it. 'Looking for trouble,' as Muff would say. Not that she *was* guilty, of course. Except in the sense that knowledge was guilt.

Muff said, 'That's better. You look better now, darling. Just a funny turn, I expect. When I was your age, I used to get them sometimes.'

*

Pansy wrote:

Dear Mother,

    I was so glad to have your long, cheerful letter about life in Islington which seems, as you say, to be full of quaint characters. I shall look forward to meeting the 'Ancient Mariner' in the holidays and the cat, Balthazar, and I hope we shall be able to go to Brighton and see Aimee's baby. I shall enjoy being an Aunt. I have put my nephew's birthday down in my Birthday Book.

    I hope you will manage to find a job soon. It is a pity that you are not trained for anything, but that is not your fault, but the fault of society. Moira Harvester, who is our Dormitory Leader this term, says it is really extraordinary how much the world has changed since our mothers were young. When you were our age, she says, girls were still brought up to believe that it was really unnecessary for them to have a career because their husbands would provide for them. It will be different for us. I have decided to become a management consultant (Moira thinks that will suit me because I am such a good organiser) and I shall make sure I have a good job before I start having my children so that I can be independent. I would like to have two children, a girl and a boy, but I am not at all sure that I want to get married. Moira is shocked when I say this, but she is old-fashioned in some ways!

    Perhaps, if you can't manage to find a fulfilling job, you ought to think about getting married again. Father is going to, as I expect he has told you. I must admit, when he wrote and told me, I was offended on your behalf, though I am getting over it now.

    Thank you for saying that Janet Morris can come to stay in the Christmas holidays. If it is all the same to you, I would rather invite Moira Harvester. It was nice of Janet Morris's parents to have me to stay at half term but it rained too hard to visit Maiden Castle and look at the earthworks, and all we did was make coconut ice and watch television. Moira Harvester has much wider interests than Janet Morris, she likes going to the theatre and discussing politics, and we have, altogether, much more in common! I think you will like her. She is very tall and quite thin.

My Bear, who is sitting beside me as I write this, sends his kind regards to you. (!) And I, Pansy Starr, send my love!
P.S. Of course I don't mean that you should rush into marriage! After all, once you have faced up to it, you might find that you quite enjoyed earning your living! Moira Harvester, who is quite good at psychology, has looked at your photograph and says that in her opinion you have a lot of potential that you haven't explored yet. And she says (though of course this is nothing to do with psychology!) that you look very young for your age!

Pansy's letter was waiting for Bridie when she came back from Eaton Square. She read it, sitting in Miss Lacey's kitchen, warming herself in front of the gas stove. Balthazar purred on her lap. He had run to her as soon as she came in the door, mewing his welcome. He had not touched the saucers of food she had left him. She tickled his ears and said, 'Poor old puss, were you lonely, all this long day?'

It was midnight, but she still felt wide awake, full of energy. Full of love – for Pansy, for the old cat who had been pining for her, for Philip . . .

She told herself that she was only falling in love because her situation had pre-disposed her to falling in love, had set a trap for her, and that, for this reason, she ought to resist it, but she knew that she did not intend to resist it. She could do what she liked, she thought. Life stretched in front of her, full of sweet possibilities. She was free to choose and wise enough, now, to keep out of any trap lying in wait for her. She laughed as she pushed the cat off her lap and said, 'Free as a bird, Balthazar,

and young, too! That's what my dear daughter says! Young for
my age and full of potential!'

Chapter Nine

'I 'm twenty-nine,' Philip said. 'Why, is it important?'

He widened his eyes with amusement – not at her question, she thought, but at the absurd, abrupt, childish way she had suddenly asked it, blurting it out between mouthfuls of hot onion soup into the first silence that had fallen between them.

'No. No, of course not!' Shamed by this lie (she had feared he was younger) she blushed and embellished it. 'I suppose I was just thinking of ages. Something to do with all those old people last night. My parents, my aunts. All born, more or less, at the turn of the century. What I was thinking was, *when* you were born must affect you . . .' She took another mouthful of soup, swallowed it, and said, bravely, 'I'm thirty-two. A war baby.'

'The war can't have affected you much. You can hardly have known much about it.'

'I was a war *orphan*! My parents adopted me.'

'Oh, I see.'

'That is . . .' Bridie began, and stopped. She really couldn't go on. Not now. Not *yet*, anyway. It would take too long and there was too much to tell. She had discovered her past – recovered it, like reclaiming land from the sea – and although what she had found was naturally interesting to her, it might not be of much interest to Philip. Even if, in one way, she felt she had known him all her life long, in another, he was still a stranger. It was a peculiar sensation, this feeling of intimacy with someone you barely knew. Exciting, she thought, looking at him sitting opposite her in this small, discreet, basement restaurant where the waiters were dressed like French matelots and bunches of herbs hung over the archway that led to the kitchen. Exciting, and faintly, pleasantly, frightening.

Philip said, 'Yes?', expectantly, and, embarrassed, she looked beyond him, at the small bar and at the menu chalked up on a blackboard. It was quite cheap, she was glad to see for his sake, though the food so far had been excellent. The thick onion soup and the fresh, crisp, white bread. She wondered if the place was in the Good Food Guide. And remembered her last meal with James . . .

'Why are you smiling?' Philip said – oddly, it might seem to an objective observer, since they had been smiling at each other almost continually in the half hour or so they had been here. But of course, she thought, the way she was smiling now was quite different.

'*Was* I smiling?' she asked, disingenuously. She could hardly tell him that her husband had taken her to a much more expensive restaurant than this on their last evening together, and then complained when he was given the bill! Philip might think that she thought *he* was mean! She said, greedily wiping up the last of the soup with a large crust of bread,'I suppose I was thinking about my family. My father and his sisters. Aunt Florence, Aunt Blodwen. Last night at dinner they were all being so kind to each other, on their best behaviour, but you could tell it was only a temporary lull in the battle. They do love each other, but what really binds them is a kind of long ago *passion*. Memories of old fights and old grudges. That's what holds them together. Perhaps it's the only way they know to express their affection. All the years that they've lived, the changes they've seen, and yet they don't seem to have changed inside, really.'

Philip said, 'Old people are just young people trapped inside old bodies. I'm afraid that isn't original. I read it somewhere.

But while we're on the subject, you don't look thirty two. I would have said so at once, as soon as you mentioned it, but I was afraid you would think I was just being gallant. But then I thought, if I *don't* say it, you might think I thought you looked older!'

She laughed, at him, and with him. Oh, he was *lovely*, she thought. She said, 'You always say just the right thing.'

'I try to please,' he said modestly. He looked at her, pushing his glasses up on his nose. 'Though not always. Not everybody.'

'You please me,' she said. She was astonished to hear herself making this bold, unequivocal statement, and relieved when the waiter came, at that moment, to remove their soup plates.

Philip said, 'I'm glad.'

There was a silence. They looked at each other. The waiter poured a little wine into Philip's glass. He sipped it and nodded. The waiter filled both their glasses.

Philip said, 'I once had lunch with a man who said the wine was disgusting. He sent for the head waiter who was very superior and condescending until he tasted it, too. Then he spat it out . . .'

'It must have been awful. This is very good, though.'

'Yes.' Philip looked at his glass. 'That was meant to be a funny story. I'm sorry, I didn't tell it very well. I suppose I'm just nervous. You know, all day I've been terrified! In case something went wrong. You might have forgotten the name of this place, or the street. I should have made sure that you wrote it down. But then I thought of worse things. There was an old film – I can't remember what it was called, but it kept coming back to me. I saw it on television, the late night movie. Cary Grant was in it, and Ingrid Bergman. They fell in love on a boat, on a trans-Atlantic crossing, but for some reason they couldn't . . .' He laughed. 'Well, anyway, they arranged to meet a year later on the top of the Empire State building. *He* was there, Cary Grant, but *she* was run over, crossing the road . . .' He laughed again, watching her.

'What would you have done if I hadn't turned up?'

'Waited. Telephoned. Scoured the hospitals. Gone to the police.'

'Would you *really*?'

'Yes, I think so. Since I'd been remembering that stupid film. Though why I say *stupid* film, I don't know. It made me cry at the time. And, if you hadn't come, it would have been useful. Reminding me that there might be some reason. Apart from your simply not wanting to see me, I mean. Fiction often is useful in that sort of way. Preparing you for things that could happen.'

'Life is much odder, though.' She hesitated, then said, in a rush, 'I suppose what I mean is that *my* life has been a bit odd just lately. I met my mother the other day. I mean, my real mother. I mean, for the first time. If I'd been relying on fiction, I would have expected something exciting to have come of that, some great revelation. Instead, there was nothing. I mean, I felt nothing.'

'What was she like?'

She shrugged her shoulders and laughed. 'Oh, a merry old party! But nothing to *me*! She gave me a lot of whisky to drink, and my half-sister's telephone number. I might ring her up. I don't know. After all, what would we have to say to each other?'

'You can't tell, ' Philip said. He was watching her gravely. She knew she had sounded uneasily flippant. Perhaps he suspected that she was not being quite honest. Well, she wasn't, she thought. Seeing Hermione hadn't meant much, not as much as she'd hoped, maybe, but it hadn't meant *nothing*. She thought of her father, and blushed. She said, very quickly, 'Sorry. I've been hogging the conversation. Me and my family . . .'

'I like it,' he said. 'I like to listen to you.'

'Really?'

'Yes, really.' He was smiling at her so sweetly, it made her feel dizzy. He said, 'Tell me – let me think! There's so much I don't know that I want to know that it's hard to know where to start.' He laughed – at himself, at this clumsy phrasing – and screwed his eyes up. Then he opened them, wide and blue. 'For example,' he said. 'Do you like travelling?'

She loved him for asking this question, for sensing her sudden discomfort, and for knowing just how to deal with it. Oh, he was kind! Kind and clever! Yes, she *loved* travelling, she cried, beaming at him with gratitude. Of course, when the children were young, her step-children, and her own daughter, they had spent most of their holidays at the seaside, in England, but these last few years, she and James (it was easy to talk about James in this context, which was another reason to be grateful to Philip for suggesting such a safe, neutral topic!) had gone abroad quite a bit. All the usual places, France, Italy, Greece — but last year James had decided that he wanted to be more adventurous and they had gone to the Soviet Union.

They had flown to Kiev, then to Tbilisi, and crossed the Caucasus in a tour bus. It had been a tiring and sometimes uncomfortable journey, all those long, jolting hours in the bus, but Georgia was a beautiful country: snow-capped mountains, rich valleys, and green, fertile plains. Dull acres of collective farms, naturally, but little private farms, too, where the people grew vines and tomatoes and fruit, and the domestic animals, the cows and the geese and the pigs, roamed as free as if they lived in the Garden of Eden. The Georgian pigs had been particularly enchanting (at least, they had enchanted Bridie), so jolly and friendly and clean, running up to the tourists and wagging their surprisingly long, curly tails like dear little dogs. But the best thing, the thing she would always remember, was the old bath house in Tbilisi that Pushkin had written about and where Lermontov (so James had told her, Bridie said, careful to give him this credit) used to go to ease his arthritic knee. It had been difficult to find at first, the Intourist guide had been unwilling to direct them to this old, tumble-down part of the city which he considered, presumably, a disgrace to the Soviet Union, but James had found a taxi driver who understood his elementary Russian and they had got there at last. Bridie had been given a bath in a vaulted, tiled cellar by a large lady in a white, nylon petticoat who had sat her down on a worn, marble slab and thrown buckets of hot, sulphurous water at her and scrubbed her down with a rough glove and a bar of coarse soap – even behind her ears and between her toes! 'It was like being a baby again, and being bathed by one's mother,' Bridie said, laughing, happy to see that Philip was laughing too, at this anecdote, and glad that she had not only managed to speak about James so calmly and pleasantly, but also to think about him, in her heart, without anger. It was a relief to discover that their life had not, after all, been unrelieved gloom; that there had been an oasis or two in the desert . . .

She smiled benignly at Philip, and at the waiter who brought them their main course. Tiny, pink, lamb chops, pale twirls of creamed potato and a tossed, garlicky salad.

'Don't overdo the potatoes,' Philip said. 'Keep a space for the cheese. Did I tell you the cheese board in this place really is something special?'

'Yes. I remember. I remember everything that you've told me.'

'Everything?'

She nodded.

'Goodness me!'

They grinned at each other. He said, 'Do you know, it's extraordinary, but last year I went to Georgia, too! Only in America, not the Soviet Union. I have an aunt in Atlanta, my mother's sister. She was ill – dying, actually, which was why I went with my mother to visit her. And, for the same reason, I didn't see much of the country, except Atlanta itself, which is just a big, rich, modern city. But it seems a coincidence.'

Bridie said eagerly, 'That's what I mean about life being odder than fiction. Full of that sort of thing! Both of us going to Georgia. Then meeting at London Airport!'

'That wasn't such a coincidence. After all, think of the times you meet people at airports! I mean, half the time, *most* of the time, really, when that happens you simply don't notice. When it isn't important. Just old so-and-so you haven't seen for a long time. You just say, good heavens, that's old Phineas Blenkin-sop, and forget all about it.'

He put his fork into a lamb chop and sighed. 'You know, it's a funny thing, but I'm not awfully hungry.'

'Too much onion soup. It was very filling.'

'Mmm. Though I don't really think that's why I'm not hungry!'

He put his hand out, touched hers, then withdrew it.

She said, suddenly flustered, 'What were you doing at Heathrow, anyway?'

'Seeing my parents off. I'd driven them up from Shropshire at the weekend. They were flying to Rome.'

'For a holiday? It'll be a bit cold, won't it, Rome in November? Though I suppose they couldn't go in the summer. I mean, running a farm.'

'Oh, it's not that. My brother does most of the work now. They always go in November, for my grandmother's birthday. She's a bit of an old matriarch and there is always a tremendous family gathering. I usually go but this year it was difficult. One of our partners is ill. I'm glad, really. Not that he's ill, of course, but that I had to stay. As things have turned out.'

He spoke softly and meaningfully. Bridie felt shy. She stirred her food round on her plate.

She said, 'Your family seem very scattered. Your aunt in America. Has she lived in Rome long? I mean, your grand-mother?'

'My aunt married an American soldier after the war. She was a G.I. bride. My grandmother has lived in Rome most of her life. Though she was born in Verona.'

'Oh?'

'Why so surprised?'

'Well. Newhouse is hardly an Italian name, is it? That's your father's name, isn't it? Newhouse. John Newhouse.'

Philip laughed. 'I'm sorry, how silly. I suppose I thought that I'd told you. My father changed his name when he settled in England. I imagine he thought he could hardly be a farmer in

Shropshire with a name like Giovanni Mario Casanova!'

Bridie looked at him.

Philip said, 'Especially at that time, just after the war. And in his situation. He had been a prisoner, sent out to work on a farm. After the war he stayed on, as a lot of Italians did, and married the farmer's daughter.'

Bridie said, 'You don't look Italian.'

'I take after my mother.'

'Was she Welsh?'

'No. English. A Shropshire Lass called Elizabeth Dobson.'

'Ah!' Bridie said.

Philip smiled at her brightly. She made herself smile back at him although her pulse was beating so wildly it made her feel faint.

He said, 'So you see, in a sense, I'm a war baby, too! If it hadn't been for the war, they would never have met, my mother and father. And we wouldn't be sitting here.'

'No,' Bridie said.

'Well, we might, of course, only it would be different. We would be different.'

'Yes,' Bridie said.

'It makes you think, don't it?' For some reason – puzzled, perhaps, by Bridie's monosyllabic responses – Philip had assumed a stage cockney accent. He waited a second or two, then went on, in his normal voice, 'If it hadn't been for my father's family, I would probably never have thought of going into the law. My grandfather was a lawyer. Rather a well known anti-Fascist. He spent most of the war in jail. That impressed me when I was young. And of course, it was why my father never got a commission in the Italian Army, which was lucky for *me*, because if he had been an officer, he would never have been sent out from the prison camp to live on a farm.'

Bridie smiled weakly. Philip was watching her. She ought to say something.

She said, 'It's a funny thing. The reason I was driving round Shropshire, one of the reasons, was that my mother lived there during the war with an old aunt. Not very far from your farm. As a matter of fact, I think she remembers some people called Dobson . . .'

Only too well, Bridie thought. Her mind raced ahead. She saw herself introducing Philip to Muff. 'This is Philip, Muff darling. The son of one of the Dobson girls on the farm.'

Philip said, 'How amazing!'

'Yes, isn't it?' Bridie heard herself give a sharp, canary-like trill of laughter. It sounded so false to her, she was sure Philip must notice, but he only looked interested. Bridie said, 'The aunt used to breed dogs. Well, she did at one time. This aunt, that my mother stayed with. I never knew her, she died in 1943, before I was born. But your grandparents, your English grandparents, I mean, might remember her.'

'They're dead. My mother might, but she would have been young then, of course. She was only seventeen when she married my father. So she might not remember.'

Muff would remember *her*, though! Elizabeth Dobson, who had, so Muff said, sometimes looked after Hermione's children.

'I'd like you to meet my parents,' Philip said. 'Would you come down to Shropshire one weekend? When they come back from Rome. I think that you'd like them.'

'I'm sure I would.'

'In the meantime . . .' Philip put out his hand and she took it. She looked at their joined hands on the white tablecloth, surrounded by small pellets of bread, and tried to stop herself trembling.

There was no way out she could see. Unless she could bring herself to tell him now, *quickly*. But what could she say? My mother, my adopted mother, that is, will believe that you are my half-brother, because of the lie that my real mother told her!

It was simply too *weird*, she thought. Presumptuous, too – as if she assumed that Philip was going to ask her to marry him. Well, she did assume that, but it was too early to say so. And yet, quite soon, it would be too late. He was honest and open. He would think it strange that she had kept this weird story from him; been so dishonest and secretive. But it wasn't her secret . . .

Philip pressed her hand, then released it, and started to eat his lamb chops. She looked at him, innocently eating, and locked her shaking hands in her lap. She said, astonished to find her voice sounding quite level and calm, 'You must meet my parents, too. Only my mother is not very well at the moment. All the family comings and goings have been terribly tiring for her. And she has a bad heart.'

Of course, if Muff died, there would be no further problem. It was only for Muff's sake she had to keep her mouth shut. As her father had done all these years. But I love Muff, she thought, horrified. How could she even *think* of her death like this – as a kind of convenience! Perhaps Philip's parents would die, instead. A plane crash, flying home. Oh, that was worse, in a way. To hope for the death of two total strangers. Particularly since they were not strangers to Philip. And it wouldn't help, anyway. If she married Philip, Muff would want to know about his mother and father . . .

Philip said, 'I'm sorry your mother's not well. I'd love to meet her when she is better. All your family. Your daughter, your father . . .' He looked at her plate and added, in a concerned voice, 'Aren't you hungry?'

'I was just thinking.' Bridie picked up her knife and fork. She said, to distract him, 'My father's a psychiatrist. Martin Mudd.'

'That's a *name*,' Philip said. 'Didn't he write that book on the connexion between drug abuse and mental illness?'

'Yes.'

'I haven't read it, but I know *of* it. I mean, it's a famous book.'

'Rather heavy going, I think, for a layman.'

'Perhaps I should try, though, before I meet him.'

'Well, of course, he'd be flattered. I don't mean in a silly way. He's a nice man.'

An inadequate word, Bridie thought. A good man, a brave man, a kind man who loved his wife and had protected her and her happiness in the way he thought best, accepting what must sometimes have seemed an intolerable burden (and worse: a degrading, farcical folly) in order to do what he felt was required of him. She could not let him down. There was a time to speak and a time to keep silent, as it said in the Bible, and silence (for her father's sake even more than for Muff's) was her only course now.

Silence and cunning. It was unfortunate that she had told Philip that Muff had known the Dobsons. Though, presumably, if and when he met Muff (and she would put off that meeting as long as possible) it would come out, anyway. She would have to warn Philip without telling him the whole truth. After all, for Muff, that part of her life, the years she had lived in Shropshire, held painful memories. A sensitive young man would not wish to remind a tired, sick old woman of the death of her aunt, the death of her daughter.

The harder thing (if she did marry Philip) would be to keep the two sets of parents apart. She could not see how to manage that yet, but she knew she would manage somehow, think of something, some story. Perhaps she had inherited some of Hermione's talent, although it was her father she felt closest to. She was conscious that the challenge exhilarated her, and, as she began to eat her chops with increasing appetite, it crossed her mind that what she had thought of as an intolerable burden might not, in fact, have been intolerable at all to her father, but had added spice to his marriage. Intrigues and evasions and secrets were what his family throve on; they were in his *blood* . . .

And in hers too, of course. It seemed to her, suddenly, thinking of her father's family stretching back into history and forwards into the future, that this kind of ancestral connexion could be more extending and fulfilling than any sweet, ordinary love; richer, more various, and also (showing how the same patterns, the same situations, were repeated in each generation, and how each generation survived them) more lastingly comforting. She hoped that it had comforted her father on his way through the maze of deceit that had trapped him (or in which he had trapped himself) and as she explained to Philip what she had understood of her father's theories about the types of psychoses that are sometimes produced by L.S.D. and cannabis resin, she set her feet knowingly, firmly, and even cheerfully, upon the same, dark path.